The Southgate Parkway Murders

The Southgate Parkway Murders

Rainy Day Writers
Cambridge, Ohio

The Southgate Parkway Murders
ISBN-13 1463591403
ISBN-10 1463591403

CONTENTS

Acknowledgments

Take several dozen eccentric chefs from all corners of the world. Place them in a six-star resort. Sprinkle with a healthy blend of tongue-in-cheek humor that includes murder and comedic mayhem. Top off with some simple, tasty recipes and you have "The Southgate Parkway Murders," a runaway fictional novel.

The eight members of the Cambridge Rainy Day Writers have blended their imaginations and writing talents to present this colossal spoof. Players in this campy, one-of-a-kind drama exist only in the minds of the authors. The plot runs the gamut from stylish writing to intentional tackiness.

We had fun putting this book together and accept full responsibility for grammatical and typographical mistakes. Our special thanks to *Mr. Lee's Restaurant*, for serving lots of hot coffee and not kicking our rowdy crowd out; to *Michael Neilson Photography*, for providing endless comedic relief and every imaginative photo in this book; to *Joy Erskine* for the endless hours she spent formatting the book, and to *The Daily and Sunday Jeffersonian* for helping get the word out to the public. A special Rainy Day thumbs-up to the following community leaders who contributed so many tasty recipes:

Colleen Wheatley, Guernsey County Recorder
Debbie Robinson, Exec. Director, Guernsey Co. Visitors & Convention Bureau
Pamela Harmon, Lifestyle/Obituary Editor, The Daily and Sunday Jeffersonian
Leslie Kleen, Ohio University Music Professor/Composer, Retired
Margo Johnston, Byesville Village Council
Daniel G. Padden, Guernsey County Prosecuting Attorney
Tony Brown, Guernsey County Auditor
Dan Beetem, Director of Animal Management, The Wilds
W. Thomas Green, O.D., Cambridge Family Eye Care
De Felt, Cambridge Pet Advocate
Janet M. Brockwell, M.D.
Dennis Dettra, Superintendent, Cambridge City Schools
Richard Wayt, Chief, Cambridge Police Department
Kay Nicolozakes, Georgetown Vineyards
Jo Sexton, President, Cambridge Area Chamber of Commerce
Ray Chorey, President and CEO, SEORMC
Tom Orr, Mayor of Cambridge
David Ellwood, Judge, Guernsey County Common Pleas Court
Dave Ogle, Scott-Ogle Realty Inc.
Jim Caldwell, Guernsey County Treasurer

Mass Confusion, Chaos in Southeastern Ohio Town

Cambridge International Airport in Gridlock (Special Associated Press Report)

The murky sky above Cambridge, Ohio, was in complete gridlock today as twelve jumbo jets circled slowly in a holding pattern, waiting to land at Cambridge International Airport. Air traffic was so heavy that the Federal Aviation Agency had been put on the alert. FAA officials were concerned because most of the jets were registered in foreign countries and many of the pilots did not have a solid command of English.

Suspicion was aroused among local, state, and federal officials when one pilot from Upper Mongolia attempted to ask which runway to use, but in the translation he apparently asked the control tower, "What is the number of flies now resting on your sister's butt?"

A Swahili pilot, in requesting the length of the runway, asked, "Do you know the way to San Jose?"

All of this had local law enforcement understandably jittery. Along with the Federal Bureau of Investigation, the Central Intelligence Agency, and the Secret Service, large contingents from Scotland Yard and Interpol are rushing to Cambridge, along with several vigilante groups from the Derwent area.

Sheriff Mark McCullum and Cambridge Police Chief Ricky Tate, both experienced law enforcement veterans, hurriedly assembled a security team that includes dozens of local officers, forty National Guardsmen, five members from Jerry Springer's security staff, volunteers from the Byesville Rotary Club, and the percussion section from the Cambridge High School Marching Band.

McCullum had little information on the jets circling his town, except that some of the biggest names in the world were aboard those planes and that their lives must be protected at all costs. Because six F-16 fighter jets, on orders from the White House, escorted the mysterious planes, McCullum's best guess was that Cambridge was to host a secret high-level security meeting. The sheriff reasoned that the only facility that could accommodate such a meeting was the gorgeous new Cambridge Ritz-Southgate, the trendy six-star hotel/resort high above Southgate Parkway.

Because the resort had been built on both city and county land, McCullum and Tate would share security responsibilities. At noon, traffic on Southgate Parkway was in gridlock as curiosity seekers flocked to the area. The Cambridge Lions Club swung into action immediately and opened an open-pit barbecue stand in the Kmart parking lot. Cambridge Rotarians got the t-shirt concession, while Kiwanians cranked up their snow cone and cotton candy machines.

"We have no idea what's going on," the head of the Cambridge Chamber of Commerce told Channel 10 from Columbus. "But whatever it is, it's bringing outside money to the area and we're ready to accommodate all visitors."

Still, long-time residents and observers are skeptical of this invasion of strangers from all corners of the earth. That attitude is best expressed by a ninety-year-old retired fertilizer salesman and a student of the human condition who said, "I don't trust none of them foreigners coming here. It can only mean trouble."

Cambridge Ritz-Southgate
To Host World's Top Chefs

Front page headline—The Daily Jeffersonian

CAMBRIDGE, O (AP)--The world's top chefs are arriving at the new Cambridge Ritz-Southgate resort, majestically overlooking beautiful Wills Creek to the north, the gleaming strands of Interstate 70 to the south, and on a clear day you can see Byesville. The gleaming high-rise resort includes one hundred suites, cheapest of which rents for $1100 per night. Windows and television are extra. Major investors are Donald Trump, Bill Gates, Warren Buffett, Bernie Madoff, and several local mini-mart operators.

Regular clientele at the Southgate include diamond moguls from South Africa, Wall Street bankers, Middle East oil tycoons, a Mexican drug cartel, Japanese MP3 executives, and millionaire sardine and herring representatives from Norway.

Saudi Arabian Sheik Muhammad Shah Abdul Hussein el al Hassid Aka Abba Al Said Udaba Uka has offered ten million dollars to the chef who creates the World's Most Delicious No-Frills Dinner. While all competing chefs are known for their exotic creations in their own homeland, the Sheik demands that they prepare only simple foods with limited ingredients with their special personal touch.

The cook-off is expected to last about a week and it is anticipated that it will inject several billions of dollars into the local economy.

Culinary experts around the world say chefs vying for the top prize will stop at NOTHING to win because, in addition to the ten million dollars, the Sheik has promised to give the first-place finisher a palace in Monte Carlo, a golf course in Malibu, a private mountain in Switzerland with an Olympic ski slope, a casino in Las Vegas, two Mercedes limousines, and four tickets to Jamboree in the Hills near St. Clairsville.

Fat's Where It's At

Jaakko Kivi arrived at the Cambridge International Airport and rushed to the limousine provided by Whiteside's, a local car dealer. There was a reason for the secrecy after his long flight from Lapland. He had demanded first class security in Cambridge because of his questionable past.

Jaakko was a renowned chef in northern Scandinavia, but in recent years he'd been a fugitive, after killing baby seals in the North Sea and heading a land swindle near his hometown of Petsamontie in a desolate region of Lapland. He'd made millions in the seal slaughter and added to his fortune after duping the Russian mafia. The Moscow underworld bought huge tracts of land from Jaakko, only to find the acreage was in the Lemmenijok National Forest and owned by the Finnish government.

More recently, he established a large company to kill reindeer and harvest their horns, which were finely ground, packed in capsules, and sold on the over-the-counter market as a spectacular aphrodisiac.

Despite the fact that it was midsummer, Jaakko wore a huge polar bear fur coat, sealskin trousers, and pink pantyhose. Standing seven feet six inches, he was an albino with pink eyes that matched his pantyhose, but he became dangerous when called "bunny." In fact, he didn't allow any sort of Easter celebration in his home.

During the short ride to the Cambridge Ritz-Southgate, the Laplander liked what he saw—dozens of fat women lined up to get into Bob Evans, McDonald's, KFC, and Burger King. What Jaakko was most attracted to, in addition to their ample girths, was their dark hair. He was tired of the blonde, blue-eyed Nordics from his home country and needed a change.

Jaakko knew he could win the simple food contest because most of his special meals were made from smoked reindeer meat, potatoes, and berry sauces. Another favorite across Norway, Sweden, Finland, and Siberia was his thinly sliced polar bear steaks, fried in seal lard and topped with a cowberry and cloudberry sauce. The sauce was used as a gravy to cover mashed potatoes which were cooked in bear fat. That was an ancient Lapp recipe, but Jaakko added a special liquor made from fermented cherries instead of the traditional vodka. He was the world's foremost expert in the use of fat and had written several books on the subject.

Three smoked reindeer had been sent from his native Renskav to Cambridge on a separate plane. The tags on the carcasses were labeled Comet, Cupid, and Blitzen. The accompanying barrel of bear lard was labeled Yogi.

Jaakko was delighted to find that the desk clerk at the Ritz-Southgate was a pleasingly overweight brunette with flashing dark eyes and three chins. He got more excited as he was shown to his suite by a pair of obese brunette hostesses of Hispanic origin. Walking behind the women, he was thrilled to see that the movement of their ample hips resembled two little boys wrestling under a blanket.

"Yes, sir," he muttered. "America is truly a wonderful country. No more bleached white Scandinavian women." He smiled to himself. What a night it would be.

The specially built hot tub in his suite was eight feet square and, unlike most hot tubs, was five feet deep to accommodate his huge frame. Jaakko's heart skipped a beat when a young Romanesque El Salvadoran woman entered his suite with fresh towels and a seductive smile on her face.

"My name is Ophelia," she murmured, eyelashes fluttering like a butterfly on a marigold.

Jaakko was thunderstruck by her beauty, quickly handing her a hundred dollar tip.

In halting English, Ophelia explained the tub operation, frequently leaning forward to brush Jaakko's chest. The sensuous, sloe-eyed Latin beauty was immediately drawn to Jaakko's snow-white skin, his glistening white hair, his pink eyes, and his resemblance to Eric the Red.

When Ophelia didn't report for work the next morning, the Ritz-Southgate management called the sheriff. At noon, a security man found the door to Jaakko's room ajar. After knocking several times, he cautiously entered to find the entire suite bathed in heavy steam. Moving to the hot tub, the security man was aghast to see Jaakko pinned to the bottom of the tub, his open eyes staring upward. He was in the grips of a fatal bear hug from the four-hundred-pound Ophelia.

The centerpiece of Jaakko's life had been his skillful use of fat, but in the end, it was fat that did him in.

****POLICE REPORT****

Guernsey County Sheriff Mark McCullum had never seen a hot tub double death before. Not that the demise of Jaakko and Ophelia was so gruesome, but because the corpses looked like overripe prunes.

This also marked the first time he'd ever seen a double death where both victims had smiles on their faces. McCullum was puzzled when Ophelia's body showed traces of some sort of animal grease. None of this made sense—smiling victims and grease.

"At first blush, this looks like an accidental death," Dr. Jane Brickwall, the coroner, mused. "Some sort of game that got out of control."

But the sheriff wasn't sure he was dealing with hot tub hanky-panky. Jaakko was in town for the cook-off and McCullum was aware, and suspicious, of some strange characters roaming the Ritz-Southgate premises. The extra long pink panty hose collection in Jaakko's dresser drawer only complicated matters.

An outside security man reported that he had seen someone wearing dark clothes, sunglasses, and a wide-brimmed hat exiting a rear door at four o'clock, two hours before dawn. He didn't know if it was a man or a woman, but noted that it was manlike in stature, but moved like a woman.

"You know, kinda ran like a sissy," the security man said. "Sort of reminded me of the police officer with the Village People."

McCullum shook his head. What was baffling was that the intruder wore sunglasses. It was pitch black outside. *So, we have a seven-foot dead guy, a four-hundred-pound dead woman, lots of grease, and a killer running around like a sissy wearing sunglasses in the dark of night*, McCullum mused.

He led his deputy to the door. "Come, Watson," he said. "The game's afoot."

"I love it when you say that," the deputy grinned.

DIVA'S DEMISE IS A RACY SURPRISE

Wilma Shortzfall dropped her toe stop a little too abruptly to the pavement and flipped like a burger in a fast food joint. She landed on her skates, but whirled in an uncontrollable pirouette, her short pink pettiskirt spinning like a hovering UFO above ruffled silver hot pants and black thigh-high fishnet stockings. Crashing hard through the polished glass doors of the Cambridge Ritz-Southgate hotel, she somersaulted agilely to her feet and readjusted the line in her stocking, all in one fluid motion.

Completely unfazed, she spit half a tooth into her hand, yanked off an elbow protector, and wiped blood off the entryway with a tattooed forearm before speed-skating to the front desk.

"Hey, you!" she buttonholed the desk clerk. "I'm here for the big cook-off. Where's the Sheik?" she brayed. "I hope he ain't no ugly lug. I like my men fast and handsome. Hmm, *you're* kinda cute." She batted her long fake eyelashes at the clerk. "How 'bout showin' me to my room, Honey?"

The clerk's face went ashen; he looked like he might pass out. Gathering his vanishing fortitude, he stuttered wildly, "B-b-b-bellhop! See Miss Shortzfall to Room 413, please."

"Too fast for ya, huh?" Wilma guffawed. "Sweetie, y'better get y'self some skates! I could teach ya some things you'd never forget." Displaying her broken tooth with a sigh, she added, "But right now I'm lookin' for a good dentist, so better luck next time."

Cambridge Skate Park was crowded with skateboarders when Wilma made an impromptu appearance later that Thursday evening.

Dressed in orange hot pants, a fluorescent pink t-shirt, and multi-colored leggings, she sailed in yelling, "YA READY TA RUMBLE?" and the scrimmage was on.

Perky Bones and the Cambridge City Band cocked their ears as the roar of skate wheels thundered toward the big pavilion. Senior citizens scrambled for their lives, dragging lawn chairs and walkers behind them, but Perky and the Band kept playing. A revolving ruckus of rowdy rollerbladers reeled into the pavilion to the accompaniment of "Buffalo Gals, Won't You Come Out Tonight." Then Perky just couldn't resist. He snatched a skateboard, donned a crazy hat, and sashayed into the swarm. The last time the band saw him, his signature grin flashed right behind Wilma Shortzfall's blonde pigtails.

Very late the next morning, wearing ruffled turquoise hot pants and fushia fishnet stockings, Wilma cinched a leather corset over a transparent purple peasant blouse. "Oh cripe, I buggered my nail polish," she frowned. After touching up her manicure and inspecting her newly-repaired front tooth, Wilma chugged a beer and popped a tic tac for breakfast. Then she pulled on her quads and skated flat-out through the hallways to the kitchen.

Centered in a full-size banked oval rink, her work island glistened like a precious jewel. Complete with spotlights, strobes, and roller rink soundtrack, it was a kitchen fit for a RollerDiva. Wilma savored a couple warm-up laps and ran several hot laps before getting down to business. Skating faster and faster, she grabbed ingredients and utensils on-the-fly. Sparks flashed in a wide arc behind her wheels. You could almost hear the announcer detailing the bout over the skating soundtrack. She went into a boiling, mashing, creaming, whipping frenzy as she prepared the foods on her menu. She would serve what she loved—jammers (warm-from-the-oven biscuits with jam bursting from their centers), stuffed meatballs, bacon garlic mashed potatoes, creamed peas, derby pie (a chewy chocolate and walnut delight), roller ice cream, and razzberry mint crush to wash it all down with. It was going to be a typical RollerGirlz dinner with lots of wonderful, yummy calories, but still classy, suitable for a Sheik.

"Get me some duct tape and round up that cute clerk from the front desk! He can help me make ice cream!" she bellowed at a maid passing on her way to the laundry.

In full RollerDiva mode, Wilma didn't notice the shrouded figure hidden by the black background behind the rink lights. Calculating Wilma's circuit, the figure slowly, unobtrusively, lowered a loop of black fishnet stocking from the rafters. Wilma's speed picked up. Two oblivious passes, then Wilma raced right into the noose, cinching its chokehold around her neck.

Duct tape in hand, the returning maid stood transfixed, her mouth frozen in a breathless "O." The reluctant desk clerk followed a minute behind, forced himself to peek around the corner of the kitchen door, took one look, and passed out cold.

Wilma did a slow spin in the rafters. She'd skated with her last pack and somebody called off the jam. So much for the victory lap.

****POLICE REPORT****

Police Chief Ricky Tate was the first officer on the scene. He found himself totally enamored with the RollerGirlz kitchen rink, but then his eyes fell on the glitzily-clad body hanging from the crossbeams. *Oh, no. Not Wilma Shortzfall. I've always wanted to travel to Southern California, sit in the suicide seats at the roller derby, and watch Wilma fly around the rink. She's got the best hip check in the game.* His mouth turned down in a stifled sob. *Guess I'll have to take that off my bucket list.*

"Hi, Ricky," said Guernsey County Sheriff Mark McCullum, striding up behind him. "What've we got this time?" He whistled his appreciation for the RollerGirlz setting. "Man, they really did it up for this gal. She must've been a pretty popular skater on the roller derby circuit."

"Yeah, she was a darn good skater," Tate answered sadly.

"Didn't know you were a fan, Ricky." Sheriff McCullum said, noticing the police chief's downcast expression. He put an arm around his good friend and colleague. "Sorry, old buddy. Try to think of it this way—she's gone to that great roller rink in the sky. She's joining all the roller derby legends before her. I imagine she's a real happy skater about now, don't you?"

Forensics arrived, immediately brewing up a storm of camera flashes and fingerprint dust. Ricky wiped a hand over his eyes. "It's okay, Mark. I got a little caught up in it there for a minute; she was my favorite roller derby star and all…but I'm okay now." He pulled on a brave smile as Dr. Jane Brickwall pushed through the double kitchen doors. "Jane! How's my number one coroner doing today?" She was wearing a terse expression.

"Losing a lot of beauty sleep. Two murders in quick succession don't bode well for later tonight," the dark-haired doctor sighed. "Am I to assume there might be a pattern developing here?"

"See for yourself," answered McCullum, pointing to the rafters, where Wilma still dangled like captured prey on a spider's web. "Could go either way, but I'm betting she's not up there perfecting her pirouette."

"Whoa! She's gonna have one bad case of fishnet burn. Have you guys got any good leads yet? The Coroner's Office isn't used to business being this good. Not much storage space in the morgue, you know. Getting short of toe tags too. Well, as soon as forensics has what they need, would you be a couple of good skates and get her down for me? We gotta get this roller derby on the road."

TRY PORCUPINE QUILLS FOR A THRILL

Maaki Tonaka checked into the Cambridge Ritz-Southgate with all the pomp and flourish of an experienced chef. He registered his signature meal as "Maaki's Alaskan Gosling Delight" and was assigned a room on the same floor as many of the other competing chefs. Retiring to his room, he stood looking in the full-length mirror fastened to the back of the closet door, bitterly reminiscing about his childhood.

Being the only Eskimo in the world with blue eyes and reddish-blond hair was a serious setback for a young Eskimo man. Maaki blamed this genetic aberration for his lack of social life in his home village of Imatursk, Alaska. He left home at the ripe old age of sixteen to get away from the jokes and ridicule he received from members of the opposite sex over his imperfections.

Maaki supported himself by working as a scrubber of pots and pans in various greasy spoon restaurants as he worked his way southward along the Pacific coast of Alaska, Canada, and the United States. The young Eskimo eventually made his way to Seattle.

He got a job in a place called The Diners Emporium, but was soon fired for slathering cold smoked whale blubber over everything in the kitchen, including the owner's 26-year-old spinster daughter, Minerva, although she certainly did not object. Minerva's face was so homely she had been known to stop an eight-day clock on the fourth day.

Maaki kept moving southward with each new job. Five years and 27 jobs later, he found himself working in a high-class four-star restaurant at Grand Canyon Village as a dishwasher. He was busing tables after the lunch rush when he first saw the two-page newspaper advertisement about the Sheik's Cambridge International Cook-off at the Cambridge Ritz-Southgate.

After studying the contest rules, he called his brother, Lomakta, in Imatursk, asking him to send a fresh shipment of frozen smoked whale blubber, reindeer brains, polar bear hearts and livers, moose ears, arctic fox noses, lichens and blue spruce tips. The latter were available in the states, but the quality just wasn't as good.

His signature dish was named after himself, of course. Maaki's Alaskan Gosling Delight was cold smoked whale blubber spread over roasted goslings nestled in a bed of boiled reindeer brains.

The trick was to catch the goslings just as soon as they hatched, for the best flavor. The goslings were stuffed with a pâté of polar bear heart and liver and just a pinch of ground arctic fox nose, then roasted at 400 degrees for about 12 minutes, 15 for extra crispy.

Maaki would coarsely chop 1 cup of onion, dice a whole reindeer brain, finely chop ½ cup of garlic, adding ½ cup jalapeno hot sauce and one cup of ground moose ears, and then saute until the brains were tender, about ten minutes. A one-inch layer would then be spread on a plate, two goslings placed on top, and the whole dish slathered with cold smoked whale blubber. This would be served with a side dish of pine nuts, lichens, and blue spruce tips cooked until fork tender in a dill and Vodka sauce.

Dessert was going to be his almost-famous Russian version of a Reese's Peanut Butter Cup, made by soaking blueberries in vodka for two days before pouring them over a chocolate and peanut butter mousse.

Maaki Tonaka's body was discovered the next morning by the hotel maid. His hands and feet had been tied to the four corners of the bed. A half-frozen moose ear was stuffed in his mouth and a twelve-inch section of reindeer antler was firmly imbedded in his chest. There were no obvious signs of a struggle in the room.

The Mexican maid ran screaming to the manager's office. There were some minutes of confusion and delay while the Pakistani night manager called an interpreter to translate the hysterical woman's words into English.

When the manager did get around to making the 911 call to the Sheriff's Department, the dispatcher had to call in another interpreter to translate the manager's words into English.

Two deputies were dispatched to make sure there really was a dead body at the Cambridge Ritz-Southgate. After viewing the corpse and the unusual cause of death, they called the dispatcher and verified there actually was a dead body in the hotel. The dispatcher relayed their information to Sheriff Mark McCullum.

****POLICE REPORT****

By the time the sheriff arrived at the hotel, a crowd of reporters milled noisily around in the lobby. The men and women of the press corps pushed each other for the privilege of shoving a microphone or camera in the sheriff's face, demanding answers to their asinine questions. "Was the murder sex-related?" "Was the killer an acquaintance of the dead man?" "Is an arrest imminent?" "Who is the leading suspect?"

Sheriff McCullum thought of them as a pack of jackals. *They know I haven't even been up to the crime scene and already they're demanding answers. What a bunch of idiots.*

Since the Cambridge Ritz-Southgate was situated right on the dividing line between Cambridge and Guernsey County, Police Chief Ricky Tate's detectives were included in the investigation. Coroner Jane Brickwall was called to the scene to determine time of death and other medical facts about the case prior to the extensive autopsy that would be performed later in the afternoon.

After an exhaustive investigation, Sheriff McCullum's deputies' report stated the murder weapon was a right side antler, recently cut from an Alaskan reindeer. This item is not readily available in Guernsey County, the State of Ohio, or in any of the lower forty-eight states, for that matter.

The only other viable clue was several handfuls of porcupine quills, scattered around the room as if some sort of a strange ritual had taken place. The local expert on Eskimo customs stated he had never heard of them using porcupine quills in any kind of tribal ritual. McCullum and Tate sent for Clara Pollen, former governor of Alaska and self-proclaimed expert on everything north of Chicago. They hoped she could give them some clarification on the significance of the porcupine quills in the victim's room.

In a statement to reporters, the joint task force simply noted that the murder was still under investigation and issued a call for anyone with pertinent information to please come forward.

Irish Host Becomes Toast

Patrick McKenna brushed back his reddish-blond hair with a swipe of his hand and admired the clouds through the window of the jet's first-class section.

"Aye, Ryan," he addressed his assistant. "Magnificent they are, the clouds. It's akin to looking at heaven itself."

"And heaven will be ours," replied Ryan, "once the Sheik tastes your famous dish of champ!"

Just then a beautiful brunette approached the men. "You must be Patrick McKenna," she said, extending her hand.

"Right you are, lass," Patrick answered as he arose to his entire five-feet, five-inch stature. He took the woman's hand and gently kissed it.

"I'm Rose Carlon, from *People Magazine*. I'm on my way to the Cambridge Ritz-Southgate cook-off to interview the chefs. What a lucky toss of the dice that we're on the same plane!"

"Lucky for me," flirted Patrick, "to be blessed with the company of one as beautiful as her name. Please, sit and have a drink with us."

After a couple whiskey sours, Patrick eagerly answered every question Rose asked.

"Tell me how you first developed your famous recipe for your potato dish, 'champ,'" Rose began.

"Ah, 'twas me mum's concoction, for sure. As a wee lad I would help her peel the potatoes—from our own garden, they were—and chop up the green onions. One day, Mum was about to put the milk in the pot for boiling the onions but, alas, me pappy had drunk the last of the milk. The nearest market was a kilometer away. Mum didn't drive an auto and refused to walk to the market. She was fuming mad, she was.

"I remember seeing her glaring at Pappy, who was passed out on the sofa with Guinness beer bottles in a heap on the floor next to him. Mum looked as if she could kill him, she did, but her face lit up and she said, "I have an idea!" And thus, the secret recipe for the famous McKenna champ was born. In place of milk, she used me pappy's own Guinness beer. It was delicious! She often made the dish for the socials throughout County Donegal and everyone was happier for it."

"Your restaurants in Dublin and Boston are doing very well. Any special plans, should you win the contest?" asked Rose.

"Aye," answered Patrick. "If me champ is to the Sheik's liking, I plan to build restaurants throughout Saudi Arabia and Yemen. I will name them, 'The Desert Leprechaun.' The logo will portray a grinning leprechaun astride a camel, eating a bowl of champ."

"Thank you so much for the interview," said Rose as she returned to her seat.

"She's a looker," Patrick commented to Ryan. "A colleen like that could make a man forget his woes."

An hour later, the two men had disembarked at Cambridge International Airport and were en route to the Ritz-Southgate. Their customized green limousine was a hit with the drivers on Southgate Parkway. Patrick leaned forward with excitement upon seeing a vehicle sporting a "Barnesville Shamrocks" bumper sticker.

"Will you look at that, Ryan! Barnesville Shamrocks! Who would have guessed there'd be a shamrock farm in Ohio? We must go there and buy shamrock garnishes for my champ."

Upon entering their suite on the tenth floor of the Ritz-Southgate, Patrick and Ryan gushed with delight. Emerald and mint shades of green dominated the décor, and verdant pictures of the Irish countryside graced the walls.

"Looks like a piece of Eire herself," Ryan remarked as he scanned the suite.

"Aye, and even champagne to comfort us," Patrick replied, noticing the ice bucket wrapped in green ribbon. "Begosh, there is a note on the bottle. From the Sheik, perhaps."

Patrick opened the envelope to find a daintily penned note addressed to him personally. Upon reading the note, Patrick's eyes widened and he literally jumped for joy.

"Gracious Lord, me prayers are answered!" he cheered, dancing an Irish jig upon the plush green carpet.

"What does it say?" asked Ryan, barely able to contain his excitement.

"'Tis a note from Chloe herself. Chloe!" he repeated, as if the name were magical. "She's a singer with Ireland's own *Celtic Woman*, the best musical group in the world!"

"Ah, ha!" Ryan cheered, and joined Patrick in an Irish jig.

Patrick slowed down to get his breath. "She says she is a fan of me champ and wants to meet me in the lounge at six-thirty. Oh, to be in the company of such loveliness!"

After a quick shave and a shower with Irish Spring soap, Patrick, with a bouquet of flowers "borrowed" from the suite, skipped down the hall in anticipation of the evening. As he boarded the elevator, a squishing sound echoed about him.

"Begosh and begorra!" he wailed, realizing that the elevator carpet was saturated. "It's wetter than an Irish bog in here! There be no rain today," he commented as he pushed the button for the first floor.

The entire Ritz-Southgate was plunged into darkness. The odor of burning electrical wires coursed through the hallways of the tenth floor. Patrick had been fried like one of his potatoes.

****POLICE REPORT****

Police Chief Tate and Dr. Jane Brickwall shook their heads as the ambulance crew removed Patrick's crisp remains from the charred elevator.

"I spoke with his assistant a few minutes ago. He said the poor guy was on his way to the lounge to meet one of the *Celtic Woman* singers," commented Dr. Brickwall. "She could still be waiting for him there."

Pierre Tosque, the hotel concierge, interrupted. "Excuse *moi*, but no singers from *Celtic Woman* are here at the Ritz."

Tate heaved a sigh and said, "The Southgate Killer strikes again. This guy never knew that he would get cooked before the cook-off. We've got real trouble here, Doctor."

"More than you know, Ricky," said Lt. Carleton, emerging from the stairwell. Geraldo Rivera and a Fox News crew are in the lobby. They want to talk to you."

THE BIG CONDOR SQUANDER

The yellow Stearman PT-17 biplane drifted lazy and low across west-central Guernsey County on its final approach to Cambridge International Airport. Barely fifteen minutes before sunset on a balmy late spring day, the crop duster's helmeted, open-cockpit pilot squinted to spot the town reservoir as he followed landmarks toward the assigned runway.

Behind him sat his mysterious passenger, thin, young, and almost entirely devoid of pigment, his complexion white as a ghost. Goggles notwithstanding, there was no mistaking the rider's aquiline intensity as he, too, surveyed the ground like an eagle anxious to land. Silver hair and an aviator's scarf streaming in the wind, Chef Lothar Assange looked every inch the international man of mystery he had become. The morrow, he knew, would bring his finest hour.

In order to evade Interpol at the passenger terminal, Lothar had astutely hired the affable Canton-based agricultural pilot to make a low profile entrance to the airport, discreetly taxiing aside to drop him off near the pesticide tanks at the southwest corner of the field. From there, he knew it would be just a clandestine two-mile forced march, mostly through woods, to the Cambridge Ritz-Southgate Hotel venue. Scaling fences? No problem. Dashing across I-70? Piece of cake. Avoiding entanglements with agents of international law? Priceless!

Lothar, to explain, had grown up in Australia as a member of the proud Queensland Assange clan, whose unofficial motto was "If it's not bothering someone, it's not fun!" Not content to simply mimic his cousin Julian's erstwhile tattletale habits on the playground, Lothar found great joy at a very young age in eating the illegal. A chance outback encounter with a rare ground-dwelling eastern bristlebird nest at age seven had first whetted his appetite.

Those darling little eggs were delicious! Next thing anyone knew, he was climbing the obligatory coolabah tree next to every billabong he could find, in order to pillage nests of the endangered Australian red gosshawk. A specialist in rare bird omelets, he seasoned his offerings with roastings of the equally off-limits mountain mistfrog and northern hairy-nosed wombat. Forbidden food was the best!

Though initially only on radar with the Australian Audubon Society, as an adult and chef to the world's most reclusive, antisocial billionaires, he wrought international chaos seeking out only the most endangered of delectables. Things came to a head when Lothar posted a YouTube video in which he pranced and laughed uproariously while poaching, and then really poaching, the last three yellow-breasted bunting eggs in Denmark. The country declared a national day of mourning. And so began the global manhunt.

Though fascinated with the possibility of ensnaring a yellow-bellied sapsucker while ensconced in Ohio, Lothar's contest hopes rested with the six magnificent, oval orbs tucked gently in styrofoam cases in the tucker bag slung over his shoulder. Only three days earlier, posing as a National Geographic photographer, he had convinced the head of the Peruvian National Forest Service to lend him a guide to the finest Andean Condor nests.

Snapping pictures of the occasional llama, glacier, and roadside Incan mummy for cover, he surreptitiously gathered his own delicious assortment of Andes Candies, so to speak—half a dozen eggs in all. If the world had been so cruel as to deny him the last dodo egg, or that of the last passenger pigeon, surely this was the next best thing!

"Hey! El zapato no está condicionada!" *(Your shoe is untied!)* he would tell his guide one moment, misdirecting his attention just long enough to swap out a plastic dummy egg from his knapsack for the real deal in a nest. He also used "Ver sus cremallera!" *(Check your zipper!)* twice with total success.

"Es que una tarántula en la espalda?" *(Is that a tarantula on your back?)* he finally asked his Peruvian associate when the shoe and zipper feints wore thin. That, unfortunately, was one misdirection too far. The poor fellow spun so fast he fell out of the tree, ending the condor nest pillaging spree at six. That would be enough however, Lothar thought; three for practice, three for the most wickedly delicious omelet the avian world could supply. The sheik had no idea what a lucky man he would be!

Thinking himself cleverly disguised as a "jolly swagman," Lothar waltzed up to the front desk at the Cambridge Ritz-Southgate, panting and covered with brambles. He asked for his room, reserved under his customary alias, John Quincy Adams. Unfamiliar with Australian hobo tradition, Matilda, the desk clerk, quietly assumed Mr. Adams had hitchhiked up I-77 from near Parkersburg. Handing him the key card, she smiled when he said "Thanks, mate!" Someday, she hoped, she'd understand West Virginians.

The next morning, as a distant Byesville rooster greeted the dawn, a strange chirping and clucking emanated from Mr. Adams' room. Passersby in the hallway took note, but it was not until room cleaning service arrived at half past ten that the secret of the sounds became known. A maid's scream alerted others to the scene.

The Andean condor is a scavenger. It feeds on the likes of roadkill. And so it was that six broken eggshells lay beside "Mr. Adams" as six baby condors had brunch. For the great white hunter of endangered species—in a twist of irony that would make PETA proud—the "chickens" had come home to roost. Chef Lothar Assange was dead!

**** POLICE REPORT ****

"It's murder, all right! I found a note beside the body that said 'Esta es la venganza de los cóndores!' *(This is the condors' revenge!)* These funny lookin' chickens didn't do it, but they've sure gobbled up a lot of the evidence," commented Sheriff Mark McCullum shortly after arriving at the scene. Before him, international fugitive and chef Lothar Assange lay dead, serving as a buffet lunch for six remarkably healthy, newly hatched Andean condors.

Suspiciously, a pot of water, almost completely evaporated, sat atop a glowing burner coil on the luxury room's convenience stovetop. Drawing upon his knowledge of "Waltzing Matilda," the unofficial Australian national anthem, Sheriff McCullum speculated that Assange was waiting while his billy boiled when the stroke of death occurred.

The water level in the billy, combined with the rate of evaporation in the heated pot, meant it had to have been placed there sometime after two o'clock in the morning. Though it appeared that condors had consumed critical evidence, coroner Jane Brickwall was nonetheless called to the scene to begin her investigation.

A note found in Assange's pocket indicated he had purloined six condor eggs high in the Andes three days earlier. Sheriff McCullum, an avid movie buff, stated that transport of the eggs from their cool native mountain environment to warmer climes likely caused rapid maturation of their feathered contents. "Thus," he announced with a wink, "*Three Days of the Condor* eggs was enough to cook this bad guy's goose!"

Honey Plan Stings Jamaican

Whaa gwaan? Running barefoot beside the road, a tiny young girl in tropical dress balanced a large basket on her head. Not many would expect this ebony-skinned young lady to be headed to the Cambridge Ritz-Southgate for the Cambridge International Cook-off.

Just last week in a remote village in Jamaica, Kalisa Clarke was living with her large family in a small grass hut. Her dad and brothers drove minivans transporting locals as well as tourists. In their spare time they operated a rum still and grew ganja. Bandulu, what they call fraud, was their way of life.

One afternoon, sixteen-year-old Kalisa saw a notice regarding a contest to name the best chef in Jamaica. The winner would go to the United States, where the prize was beyond belief—a palace, plus many other prizes. She quickly ran home to tell her family.

"Mammy, Daddy, there is cooking contest for United States," exclaimed the excited Kalisa.

"You no cook," said her brothers.

"But the prize be a palace! We would have beautiful place to live and rooms for everyone."

"Yea, man, we help you. No problem! We will run down the road selling the ganja. Just say, 'Hey man. This good ganja help you feel good.'"

Kalisa was not a real chef, even though she often cooked for the family. She did have one special dish they all enjoyed called dulcunu, a sweet cornmeal dumpling, boiled and wrapped in banana leaves. Add a cup of ganja tea and you have a therapy for illness as well as stress. They were a happy family but this contest could change their lives in many ways.

Next morning, she squeezed into the minivan. The arms of passengers were hanging out the windows, so it resembled an octopus. Reggae music from the radio, accompanied by beating on the sides of the van, sounded like steel drums. They headed over Gold Mountain, named for the marijuana grown there, to the contest at Montego Bay. No one was surprised when Naomi Gayle from Sandals Resorts was named the top Jamaican Chef.

But Kalisa had a devious idea. After the contest, she and two brothers captured Naomi, tied her up, and put her in the back of their van. There was an old still near their small village, a perfect hiding place.

Since Kalisa and Naomi were about the same size, it didn't take much disguise for their resemblance to be remarkable. Later, Kalisa's brother helped her stow away on a cruise ship headed to Miami. There she met her cousin, who drove a produce truck north. Everything worked like clockwork and Kalisa reached Guernsey County early on the first day of the contest.

"Cuz, drop me on Southgate Parkway by Cambridge International Airport so people don't know I come in produce truck," said Kalisa. "Then I run up Parkway to Ritz-Southgate. No problem!"

Since she wasn't a famous chef, a fresh fruit salad was her plan. In her basket, she had some ackee, mangoes, and mammy apples from the trees in their yard, plus two bottles of Jamaican rum from their still. That would add a little extra zing.

Watching near the airport, a shadowy figure sent word to the Ritz to put the "honey plan" in motion. High on the hilltop overlooking Interstate 70, the stage was being set for the latest caper.

Dressed in a red tropical flowered dress with matching red bandana around her dreadlocks, Kalisa ran barefoot up Southgate Parkway. Her basket, covered in tropical blossoms, was balanced proudly on her head. She tried to stop cars to sell them sugar cane, which she also had in her basket for snacks.

"Buy some sugar cane," she shouted. "It be sweet and good to chew. You will like." Someone gave her a dollar bill! Usually she only received coins on the roads back home.

As she approached the Ritz-Southgate parking lot, someone in canvas coveralls watched from the hilltop, ready to release another surprise to the arriving chef.

Well pleased with the beautiful delicious fruit she had purchased or stolen, Kalisa hoped to see that honey of a sheik who was giving away the palace. *I will give Sheik some ganja from my basket. When he smokes it, he will be so happy and give me all the prizes*, she thought.

Entering the parking lot, she heard a buzzing sound and saw a large dark cloud. A swarm of huge bees was suddenly overhead. The fresh fruit, or perhaps the scent of tropical flowers, sent them directly to Kalisa. The bogus Jamaican chef was fatally zapped by more than a thousand bee stings.

****POLICE REPORT****

The Guernsey County sheriff, Mark McCullum, checked the body in the Ritz-Southgate parking lot. There was no ID on the body, but Ritz management said this lady was perhaps a contestant at the cook-off.

It appeared the swarm of bees found the basket of fruit on her head very attractive and descended for some samples of both fruit and the young lady, stinging countless times. The swelling made her unrecognizable.

Her dress indicated she was perhaps from Jamaica. Her picture and prints were faxed to the Kingston police for identification, but the fingerprints did not match those of Naomi Gayle, the famous Sandals chef.

In fact, Kingston police were investigating the disappearance of said Naomi, who friends said was taken by two men and placed in a van last week.

The sheriff was a part-time beekeeper. He noted immediately that the three-inch insects found dead in Kalisa's basket were not native to Guernsey County. No, these were cliff bees from the Himalayas, largest honey bees in the world, known as apis laboriosa.

McCullum guessed that these vicious monsters were imported from the steep cliffs outside Nepal. Imported, obviously, to commit this dastardly murder.

You could hear the sound of *zzub, zzub* in the parking lot. That is the sound of a bee flying backwards to flee the scene of the crime.

Witnesses were of little help. Several said they saw someone wearing a bee veil and heavy gloves fleeing the scene in a honey-stained car bearing license plates from either New York, New Jersey, or Connecticut. Of course, they were chewing Bumble Gum.

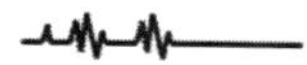

A Kielbasa Knife Can End Your Life

Gazing out the window of his gold and black 747, Lech Lipski marveled at the size of the Cambridge Ritz-Southgate resort. *It's bigger than the city*, he thought. *High government officials must live here*. Passing quickly through customs at Cambridge International Airport, he was greeted by a small contingent of "The Sons of Poland" and the local Polish-American polka band before being whisked away in a Polonez limo to the Cambridge Ritz-Southgate.

Pausing briefly at the VIP entrance to the resort, he spoke to the crowd in broken English. "I here to vin vor Poland." Waving as he went in to register, he shouted, "Polski Motsna, Dobla Notch," *("Polish Power, Good Night")*. After registering, Lech ordered two bottles of vodka, six holubky *(cabbage rolls)*, two pagachie *(flat bread stuffed with cheese)*, and twenty-four boxes of chocolate covered cherries.

Born in the Warsaw ghetto during WWII, he was the only male out of ten siblings. Lech's sisters dressed him in skirts and braided his hair until the war was over to protect him from the violence outside their home. His early childhood was traumatized by these events and the war. Hiding behind doors, he watched in horror as Nazi soldiers came for his sisters and took them away. Hours later, the girls would return bruised and crying. Lech never forgot the looks on their faces. One blond Nazi, Captain Halder, was extremely brutal.

After the war, while working in his sister's restaurant with his best friend Stephan Lechman, he discovered he had a talent for cooking. By the time he was in the tenth grade, he was their top chef.

Following high school, he and Stephan were admitted to the world famous Polish Culinary Institute. After four years he surpassed everyone, including Stephan, for the grand prize—the "Big Kielbasa" trophy and a hundred thousand złotys.

For decades, Lech traveled the world preparing his famous kielbasa recipes—kielbasa with snow peas and sweet-and-sour kielbasa. His most famous dish was General Jaruzelski kielbasa, lemon kielbasa served in guacamole sauce. While Lech's career blossomed, Stephan's plummeted to bankruptcy. Lech forgot about his lifelong friend, but he never forgot what happened to his sisters.

Several times a year, he traveled to Germany for seminars and personal appearances, after which he would slip away late at night and seek out men the approximate age of his sisters. Stalking his prey, he would pounce on them and slit their throats with a serrated kielbasa knife.

When Lech was invited to participate in the Cambridge International Cook-off, he was ecstatic. Recently, while visiting Germany, he had learned Captain Halter, now 90 years old, was living under an assumed name in Pittsburgh. Lech saw an opportunity to settle an old score.

Once settled in his suite, Lech called for his dinner to be served. "Knock loud," he told room service, "I vil be sleeping in ze Jacuzzi recliner."

Approaching Lech's suite, the bellhop noticed the door ajar. Shouting "Room service," he pushed it open.

The suite was empty and ransacked. Chocolate covered cherries were strewn about the room. Calling Lech's name, the bellhop saw the Jacuzzi recliner overturned. Moving the chair, he stared in horror at the blood covered body lying on the floor, with a pearl handled kielbasa knife embedded in the middle of his back.

Slowly backing away from the gruesome scene, he tripped over the food cart, spilling its contents on the floor. Running from the room, he screamed for someone to call security. The next few minutes were chaos as emergency vehicles and police cars raced to the scene.

****POLICE REPORT****

Entering the room, Sheriff Mark McCullum paused and stared at the heinous scene.

"What have we got, Mark?" a voice from behind him asked. Turning, Mark saw Police Chief Ricky Tate in the doorway.

"I'm flabbergasted, Ricky. We provided security fit for a king. Now this happens."

"Who is it?"

"I assume it's Lech Lepski. I never met the man. I saw him once, and that was on a TV cooking show. I believe it was *Hell's Kitchen.* I thought he was a larger man. By the way, why are you here?"

"I heard it on the scanner. Since this resort straddles the city limits, I didn't know who had jurisdiction. Actually, Mark, ah…the mayor sent me. You know how he feels about this."

"I kind of figured that," McCullum replied. "He sure was upset when that photographer from the Daily Jeffersonian found those old photos showing the resort straddling the city/county line."

"Yeah, he sure was worked up, like those reporters outside."

"Reporters?"

"Yep, there was a crowd gathering when I came in. We need to make a statement," Tate said.

When the two entered the hotel lobby, they found news teams from all the major networks were set up. Stepping up on the edge of the reptile fountain, McCullum called for quiet.

"Listen up, listen up. I will make a brief statement, then we will take a few questions. At approximately nine-ten tonight, we were notified of an apparent homicide in room 743. Arriving a few minutes later, we discovered the body of a deceased male Caucasian lying on the floor. I'll take a few questions."

"Was it Lech?"

"I'm not sure, Johnny. Why do you ask?"

"I sold him a million dollar life insurance policy last year."

"You sold Lech a million dollar life insurance policy?" Mark replied. "I didn't know he was in town last year."

"He was here for the Hoppy Festival; he dressed up as a cowboy. He was in and out of town before anyone knew it."

"How was he killed?" a reporter from the HSN asked.

"He was killed with a pearl handled kielbasa knife, the kind they sell on TV. Do you know anything about these?"

"I do, Sheriff. I'm from the Home Shopping Network, and we sold several thousand sets of these knives. As a matter of fact, we sold a set to your wife."

"Better check the knives in your kitchen drawer," a voice from the crowd said sarcastically.

"How large was the body?" a reporter from Fox News butted in.

"I'll take this one, Mark," Tate responded. "The body appears to be that of a male, approximately seventy years old and weighing one hundred ninety pounds. Do you know him?"

"I met Lech last year at the International Kielbasa Festival. He weighed around four hundred pounds and had a girth of sixty inches. The man who checked in yesterday was a small man. Lech is known for his practical jokes. Are you sure the dead man is Lech?"

"Hmm, good question," said McCullum. "He went from four hundred pounds to one hundred ninety pounds...does anyone know what's in Lech's kielbasa? Or is it Lech who is in Lech's kielbasa?"

As the Wax Worm Turns

When the invitation arrived, the news spread through Peterborough, Ontario, like a wood fire on a windy day. Clarence Skinkle had been asked to compete in the Cambridge International Cook-off competition.

Clarence was the popular owner of the famous Bait and Burger, a high-end restaurant on Little Lake, which was not to be confused with Big Lake, which was over in the next county. Whoever named the lakes in Canada apparently didn't bother with research. Short Lake was longer than Long Lake and Black Lake was very clear, while White Lake was murky.

The Bait and Burger had its beginnings as a sort of catch'em and skin'em type eatery and bait shop. As its reputation for outstanding but simple food grew and business picked up, it became necessary to replace the building with a larger, modern structure. But Clarence had never seen a need to change the name. Simple food in elegant surroundings made sense to him.

He had designed the new restaurant with a door that connected the kitchen and the bait shop, where he raised minnows, night crawlers, maggots, and wax worms. He insisted that his cooks wash their hands after placing night crawlers in little tubs for excited fishermen, but who knew?

Clarence was a tall fella with curly blonde hair, what there was of it, and twinkling blue eyes. Of French, English, and Indian heritage, he had never married, but he had been in love once, years ago.

She was an Ojibwa Indian girl, Oh-le-ta, meaning "Maid-With-One-Crossed-Eye." She and Clarence shared a great life for a while. She was a sweet little thing and not bad to look at, but he could never figure out just where she was looking.

Among other things, she had introduced him to wax worms, and a wide range of uses for the little wigglers. Not only are they very effective for walleye bait, but they serve as great filler for ground meats.

But that all ended when a slick-talking Italian gambler from Steubenville made a fishing trip to Small Lake one summer. He set eyes on Oh-le-ta and stole her away. It may have been her weird eye that threw Clarence off, thinking she was looking at him instead of the stranger. As far as he knew, they were living on the Ohio River, bobbing along on a gambling boat. That pretty much ended Clarence's faith in people in general and women in particular.

So, privately, in spite of a certain popularity with the ladies, he simply didn't believe that a woman could fall for him. No, he was sure women were interested in him only because of his burgers. After all, he had been featured in nearly every metro newspaper across Canada. *Yes*, Clarence told himself, *the burgers have to be the attraction and the reason they keep coming back to the eatery*. There were gold diggers and burger diggers and Clarence was suspicious of the latter.

When he received the invitation from Sheik Muhammad Shah Abdul Hussein el al Hassid Aka Abba Al Said Udaba Uka to vie for millions in prizes in the renowned cook-off, Clarence's thoughts immediately turned to the menu.

"I'll present for the event the meal that made me famous, the meal that made all of Peterborough famous—my pièce de résistance: burgers and frites; beef, moose or venison," he proclaimed to his staff. It was a meal that always pleased the palate, no matter how critical the customer. No flourishes, no tricks. Just freshly butchered meat, expertly grilled and accompanied by twice fried potatoes, as prepared in the Belgium fashion.

What made Clarence's burgers so special was "the personal touch." He killed the cows, deer, and moose with his homemade bow and arrows. It was a tradition some of his North American Indian ancestors followed. Clarence, while not active in tribal affairs, belonged to the Bellacoola tribe. His Indian name was Agkushla, meaning "Man-With-Fish-Eyes."

While there was no proof, rumors persisted that he tossed in a handful of wax worms when he ground his burger meat, to give it a slightly different flavor.

Clarence arrived at the Cambridge International Airport with a crate of carefully packed cooking equipment, including a large iron skillet, an equally large iron pot, several special utensils, aprons, jackets, and toques. He was very particular about his kitchenware and how it was handled. And, of course, one must be properly decked out for the presentation.

For reasons known only to himself, he also packed some deerskin Indian clothing and his handmade bow and arrows. There were plenty of deer he could shoot at Salt Fork State Park, he had been told, and he had seen several cattle grazing on a hillside not far from the Ritz-Southgate.

In his suite, Clarence checked the Yellow Pages and found a bait store near Seneca Lake. The people there promised to have ten dozen wax worms ready for him the following day. "Waxies," or bee moths, are exceptionally high in protein and calcium, but they are also fattening, so Clarence was extremely careful in blending his burger meat.

After a light meal in the resort's dining room, he returned to his suite, where he studied a map of Salt Fork State Park before dropping off to sleep. He never woke up.

****POLICE REPORT****

"It's stuff like this that makes me wonder if I should run for reelection," a shocked Sheriff Mark McCullum said as he and Police Chief Ricky Tate surveyed the scene of the crime.

Both men studied the body of Clarence Skinkle, hanging from the shower rod in the bathroom. The deceased wore only a headband with a feather in it, a loin cloth, and lots of red, yellow, and blue war paint.

"He doesn't look much like an Indian," mused Tate. "I never saw a blonde-haired Indian. But those twelve arrows sticking in his chest must mean something."

McCullum nodded. "Yes, a Canadian Indian of some kind. Notice the little maple leaf flag in his right hand. He was representing Canada in the cook-off."

"Obviously someone didn't like Canadians," Tate said. "Look at those arrowheads sticking out of his back. They're actually made of flint. Sure didn't come from Cabela's."

"This is strange," McCullum said, moving to the bed to sort through an open suitcase bearing a large Toronto Blue Jays sticker. "There are three magazines here."

"Playboy?"

"No. He subscribed to *Wax Worms for Fun and Profit*, *Maggots Mean More Money*, and *Longer, Fatter Night Crawlers in Half the Time*."

"Man, this opens up a whole new can of worms in this serial killing thing," groaned Tate.

"Yeah, there's no easy way to wiggle out of this mess," replied the sheriff.

Somebody Did Birdie Dirty

It took three letters and finally an unofficial visit from the Saudi ambassador in Ulaanbaatar, Mongolia, to convince Genghis Gansuka Tomorbaatar Kahn to enter the Cambridge International Cook-off. Kahn finally agreed to make the trip, provided he could tell his story on The Jerry Springer Show.

Springer producers jumped at the chance because Kahn had been married to five different women—a Siberian bounty hunter, a whaler from a remote island in the Bering Sea, a Japanese Geisha girl, a Chinese diesel mechanic, and Miss Mongolia 2005.

The Saudis, through some close ties with the White House, made all the arrangements for the Springer show and even got him the job of hosting one episode of Saturday Night Live.

As for the cook-off, Kahn's culinary skills were well-known in Russia and Asia, but he'd been reluctant to spend much time away from Mongolia, where he was something of a folk hero. A direct descendent of thirteenth century Mongol warlord Genghis Kahn, his name translated into "Steel Ax," though he preferred to be called "Birdie" for some unknown reason.

He became wealthy at an early age after establishing a large chain of roadside eateries across Mongolia and Siberia, housed in circular animal skin tents called yurts. These collapsible tents have been used for thousands of years by Mongolian nomads. The tiny roadside cafés were popular because of Birdie's Brew, a steaming tea-like mixture of high-grade cream from mare's milk, a special Chinese black tea, and Russian vodka. That was a daytime drink. In the evening, for the supper crowd, Birdie added a dollop of goat fat, barley balls, and mutton chunks, transforming the tea into a delicious soup.

On his several ranches, Birdie continued to increase his yak herds. He had managed somehow to make yak meat taste much like the McDonald's Quarter Pounder. Last year, he expanded and changed the name of his tiny cafés from Birdie's Yurts to Home of the Big Yak. The motto on all outside signs said *"Try a Sack of the Big Yak. You'll Never Ask for Your Money Back.*" His yurts profits doubled overnight and Birdie made plans to expand to Burma and Tibet.

The small plane landed unceremoniously at Cambridge International, but before he checked in at the Cambridge Ritz-Southgate, Birdie asked his driver from Dunning Motors to make several stops. Grabbing a newspaper from the box in front of the Daily Jeffersonian, he scanned the "Livestock for Sale" ads, looking for goats. After that, he checked briefly with a stable to inquire about a donkey. From a cell phone in the limo, Birdie called The Wilds, where he was told they could not sell him a camel and llamas were out of season.

Birdie was disappointed. Now he'd have to change his menu for the cook-off. He'd serve a split sheep's head, using the skull as a bowl, and sweeten the brains with raisins soaked in sake, which also made the eyeballs clear and inviting. It was a simple, easy-to-prepare meal.

While his ancestors were savage looters, plunderers, and killers, Birdie was basically a quiet, handsome man. Housekeepers at the Cambridge Ritz-Southgate were surprised that he had brought with him several life-size cardboard cutouts of himself as an Elvis impersonator, as well as many large photos of Whoopi Goldberg, for whom Birdie secretly lusted. They also noticed the wigs and fake Elvis sideburns on the bathroom counter, along with a Delta airline ticket to Memphis.

After a light dinner of peanut butter and banana sandwiches (Elvis' favorite snack), he donned his sequined jumpsuit and Elvis glasses, then took a stroll to get the feel of the opulent hotel. It was Karaoke Night in the crowded lounge. Birdie patiently waited his turn while a half dozen locals failed miserably to put across a plethora of country songs. An hour later, he took the microphone and within seconds was wailing in Mongolian:

"The warden threw a party in the county jail,
Prison band was there and they began to wail.
Band was jumpin' and the joint began to swing,
Should'a heard those knocked out jail birds sing.
Let's Rock! Everybody let's Rock!
Everybody in the whole cell block,
Was a-dancin' to the Jailhouse Rock!"

Lounge customers trampled each other to get to the dance floor to gyrate crazily to the music. Women moaned; men convulsed uncontrollably when Birdie belted out "It's Alright, Baby." Everyone was rocking.

Everyone but one person—the character in the wide-brimmed hat and sunglasses seated behind the potted palm tree at the rear, contempt contorting the evil, twisted lips.

When Birdie failed to show up at a meeting of all the competing chefs the next morning, a cook-off official went to his room. There, sprawled on the floor, was Birdie, his gold lamé jumpsuit soaked in blood. There was no doubt that Birdie would never get to Graceland.

****POLICE REPORT****

The staff at the Ritz-Southgate was on edge as rumors flew about the resort. Police had released little information to the press, but gruesome accounts of the murders circulated from the parking lot valets to the housekeeping department. The stories got more hideous with each telling. Most employees hoped the cook-off would be cancelled and the Sheik sent packing. One desk clerk said, “I felt safer when the Mafia convention was here last week than I do now. These foreigners give me the creeps.”

“I’ve never seen so many uniforms and shiny badges,” one groundskeeper lamented. “If this keeps up I’m going back to my old job at the Salt Fork Golf Course. Nothing ever happens out there.

Police Chief Ricky Tate, who hadn’t slept in three days, shook his head as he surveyed the blood-spattered body. Without a doubt, a serial killer was on the loose at this five-star resort and the strain was beginning to show on every member of law enforcement. Bodies were piling up and the city was being overrun by strange people wearing strange clothing.

“Holy smoke,” Tate muttered. “A Mongolian Elvis? Who’s going to believe this?”

“I caught his act in the lounge last night,” said Detective Jim Todd, himself a Johnny Cash impersonator. “He was pretty good.”

“There’s no doubt as to how he died,” Tate said measuredly. “All these cuts and lacerations about the head were done with that pair of blue suede shoes with the metal heel plates.”

Todd shook his head sadly. “Elvis is definitely leaving the building—feet first.”

GALLONS OF MACALLAN'S

Angus McHeilancoo tripped, almost kissing the tarmac as he stumbled off the Sheik's Piper Malibu at Cambridge International Airport. This was his first foray into America. He hated to fly these days, but the prize list for the Cambridge International Cook-off was an irresistible lure to his native Scottish sensibilities.

The chartered flight from Craigellachie to Columbus had been well-stocked with his favorite Macallan Scotch whisky, "the water o' life," as he referred to it. Angus, at first, tipped just a wee dram to calm his traveling nerves, then another, followed by another. It was a long, fluid flight.

"Here, let me help ye." Callum, his apprentice, materialized at his elbow. "Ye'll be needin' yer bed at the Southgate Ritz-Cambridge Hotel, I'm thinkin'."

Angus suddenly reeled backwards and stared in boozy dismay at something only he could see blocking the walkway ahead of him—a shaggy green dog the size of a cow, with a braided tail, its teeth bared menacingly.

"Gi' 'way, Cu Sith *(pronounced coo-shee')*," he bellowed. "Gi' oot o' me way, ye faery dog." He swayed precariously, growling in response to the snarls of the invisible hound.

"What mean ye, Angus? Cu Sith isnae here. 'Tis only me, Callum. Here, let me…"

"Dinnae fash yersel'." Angus waved Callum off, strutting clumsily onward. "I can walk me ainsel'."

Callum rolled his eyes wearily. Resuming his customary position behind Angus, he followed close, just in case.

"Oh, me pur heid," Angus moaned as the light of day scattered across his pillow the next morning. Well-accustomed to such after-effects, he crowed, "But I know just the thing. Gi' me a hair o' the dog wha bit me and I'll be fightin' fit again." He poured a dram as he ordered pork and beans on toast and sausages from room service, then slipped on a pair of loose trousers. When breakfast arrived, he ate ravenously and washed it down with Macallan's.

After an invigorating hot shower, he dressed in his McHeilancoo kilt and a cream-colored Ghillie shirt. Thick and muscular, with unruly red hair and mischievous twinkling green eyes, Angus was a fine specimen of Scottish manhood.

Filling his flask with Macallan's and tucking it handily into his sporran, he called for his limo. Tee time was 10:00 a.m. Anxious to meet his American hosts at the clubhouse beforehand, he knocked sharply on Callum's door as he passed. "I'm off tae the links," he bellowed. "Mind yer ready wi' me kitchen by half-two," he instructed sharply. "We'll start wi' the soup and beef."

"Aye, Angus. I'll have things ready fer ye. Nae worries," the yawning voice of the apprentice assured him.

At the Cambridge Country Club, Angus was greeted heartily by new American friends Strom Roarr, Karl Olthousand, and Shel "Dom" Seen. "Guid tae meet ye, laddies!" he whooped. "Shall I show ye how it's done?" He nodded toward the bar with a saucy grin. "We'll begin wi' a cock o' the wee finger, aye?"

"If you're buying, I'm in," laughed Karl.

"Are ye daft? I'm a Scotsman!" roared Angus with glee. He clapped Karl on the back mightily and the surprised optometrist stumbled forward, catching his spectacles as they tumbled from his face. "I cannae buy the first round and dishonor me clan. Nae. But I'm a fair man; sae if I dinnae win th'day, the whisky's on me!"

You can always tell a Scotsman," Mayor Roarr chuckled quietly in Dom's ear, "but you can't tell him much."

Dom's eyes creased into a smile. "Do you know why Scotsmen are so good at golf?" he asked. Strom shook his head no. "They know the fewer times they hit the ball, the longer it will last." Angus grinned and nodded in agreement.

After losing an amicable round of golf, always a good sport, Angus ordered the obligatory wee dram all around. The others raised a toast to his sportsmanship. Megan, the petite and perky auburn-haired barmaid, was especially attentive. Angus followed her with his eyes as she scribbled a phone number on a coaster and slipped it under his whisky with a wink. Returning to the Ritz-Southgate, Angus found it difficult to focus on the cooking competition.

But focus he must. He went straightaway to the kitchen. His menu was simple Scottish fare—first course, cheese soup and dumplings, a meal in itself. Angus had brought along his own fine Scottish cheddar, "the most important ingredient," he reminded Callum. From the dining room, the aroma elicited ecstatic sighs from the Sheik. All was going well.

When the collops of beef were tender, Callum expertly plated mashed neeps, mushy peas, and potato scones.

"Off wi' ye now, an' tak yer break," Angus directed, adding a redcurrant garnish. "Mind yer back tae serve."

As the kitchen doors swished closed behind Callum, Angus took a healthy swig of Macallan's, turning his attention to the collops. Artfully twisting the steaming meat, he added the finishing touches to the presentation. Fruit-filled dessert meringues lined the counter like silk-bedecked handmaidens waiting to serve the Queen.

The doors swished open again. "Guid. Callum, serve the collops straightaway."

Scant minutes later, Callum returned to find a grisly surprise. Splayed on the prep table, throat slit with the shards of a bloody

Macallan bottle, lay the body of the once-mighty Scottish chef. Surveying the gory proof, Callum realized Cu Sith had indeed forecasted death at the airport yesterday. Alas, there'd be nae mare whisky fer Angus.

****POLICE REPORT****

"That's some precision filleting job there," muttered Sheriff Mark McCullum, committing the murder scene to memory while the forensics guys got to work. *And with a Macallan's bottle, no less. What a waste of good whisky.*

No sign of resistance at all. No witnesses. No tell-tale artifacts either. Just a big brawny chef stretched across a table, sporting a gaping hole where his Adam's apple used to be. Whoever the perpetrator was, he was good and quick with a knife.

Abjectly, McCullum mused, *...and what was that apprentice babbling about a green dog? Ranting about 'faerie forecasts' of 'death within a fortnight.' Where do these crazies come from?*

Cursory interviews with the only people who'd seen him that day revealed that Chef McHeilancoo was a likeable enough fellow, a little rough around the edges, but a threat only to the McCallan's bottle in his hand. There seemed to be no hidden background or intrigue of any sort to point a finger in any particular direction.

We've got to get these murders solved or Scotland Yard will be crawling all over us, the sheriff worried in silence. *Worse yet, it'll make the world news headlines and we'll look like idiots. After all Mayor Roarr's done to improve Cambridge's image, how could this happen?*

He studied the murder scene one last time as forensics finished their work. *Some days it just doesn't pay to get up, does it, Angus?*

THE CLUE WAS BELOW THE TATTOO

When Phyla Dilworth tooled into the parking lot at the Cambridge Ritz-Southgate on her customized Harley low rider, she created quite a stir among the news media. She was clad from head to toe in flamingo-colored leather, complete with silver fringe down the sleeves and across the back.

The Cambridge International Cook-off committee chairman had her fill out a registration card that included her signature dinner. She listed the main course as braised mountain oysters au gratin. Since most of the reporters covering the entry booth had no idea what mountain oysters were, she breezed right through that part and was assigned a room on the same floor as many of the other chefs.

As Phyla paraded through the lobby of the hotel, her confidence was at an all-time high. After all, she had been the head chef at Deadwood Dick's Saloon and Eatery in Deadwood, South Dakota, for two years. Despite what those mental midgets from the health department said, she was definitely not responsible for all those tourists getting food poisoning.

She was proud of the fact she had shot two of the jerks in the melee which ensued when they tried to close the place. Those sissy tourists were probably already sick when they came in to Deadwood Dick's. Those kinds of people were always looking for someone to blame for their own mistakes.

She was willing to bet none of the other cook-off participants had been voted "Inmate Chef of the Year" for two years running at the Deer Lodge State Prison in Deer Lodge, Montana. The first year, she had blown away her competition with her version of road-killed antelope and buffalo boudin stew. The second year, she won easily with her special barbequed buzzard wings and mac 'n cheese over burro chops.

Phyla was five-feet-four and weighed two-sixty-five with long blonde hair, usually worn in a modified cornrow style. She sported three tattoos of the type normally worn by inmates of various penal systems. The skull and crossbones on her right forearm meant she had killed someone. A miniature devil with "Born to raise Hell" on her left leg signified she was a member in good standing of the Tasmanian Road Devils Motorcycle Club. The heart with "Kiss My Grits" inside it, tattooed just below her navel, had a special personal meaning known only to Phyla.

She figured she could use the ten million dollars, the palace, and limos, and just maybe she could talk the Sheik into taking the fourteen-year-old-girls in on a trade for fourteen-year-old boys instead. To her way of thinking, the only practical use for young giggly girls was as scullery maids. But young boys were entirely another matter.

Phyla decided to work on her menu before going down to the five-star restaurant for dinner. After all, this was a great opportunity for a relatively unknown chef to gain the recognition and fame necessary to succeed in the culinary world. It could very well be an important milestone in her life.

Her recipe for braised mountain oysters au gratin called for mountain oysters, three or four (per serving), depending on their size. They must be marinated in Coors beer for two days before braising. The sauce consisted of Velveeta cheese, cattail roots, rose hips, and opossum livers sautéed with a stick of butter, three cloves of garlic, and six finely chopped jalapeno peppers. This mixture was ladled over the oysters after they had been placed on a bed of mashed parsnips.

The accompanying salad ingredients were dandelion hearts, leaves from two large Canadian thistles, cilantro, chopped tomato, a tablespoon of finely chopped spearmint leaves, three cloves of elephant garlic, and two slices from a large purple onion. The dressing consisted of equal parts tequila, molasses, and WD-40. Dessert was root beer schnapps and red raspberries drizzled over lime sorbet.

With her menu completed, a shopping list done, and the oysters marinating, Phyla decided to take a nap before dressing for dinner. Before starting her nap, Phyla laid out her evening clothes. She was going to go all out for this evening's festivities and wear her favorite outfit. This was a gold lamé pants suit, a flame red blouse, and her glitter-coated eye shadow and lip-gloss. This might be considered overdressing in some quarters, but what the hey? You only live once.

When she did not answer her wake-up call, the front desk clerk sent a bellhop up to knock on her door. When she did not respond, a security officer was sent to unlock her room.

The security officer opened the door and entered the room to find a nude body stretched out on the bed with a large chef's knife protruding from a "Kiss My Grits" heart-shaped tattoo just below the navel. There was one other very apparent startling fact, Phyla Dilworth was a man.

****POLICE REPORT****

The night manager of the Ritz-Southgate, Dali Bhual, promptly reported the matter to the Cambridge Police Department. Chief Ricky Tate sent two uniformed officers to the hotel to verify the report. Once the officers reported back to the chief, he realized there was a jurisdictional problem. The line that divided the city from the county ran right down the middle of the hallway that led to the room where the murder took place.

After a lengthy conference with Sheriff Mark McCullum, it was decided to form a joint task force to investigate the gruesome murder. While the coroner, Dr. Jane Brickwall, proceeded with a thorough autopsy, city police and sheriff's deputies interviewed, fingerprinted, and photographed everyone and everything in sight.

The murder weapon was believed to be one of a matched set of knives belonging to the victim, as the rest of the set was found in the victim's room. The investigators were totally baffled as to why the victim was impersonating a woman.

It was difficult to interview several of the hotel's employees because they spoke little English. Some of the employees, believing the police were rounding up illegal aliens, had skipped out the back door as soon as the first police car pulled up at the front of the hotel.

McCullum and Tate issued this statement at a press conference: "After an extensive investigation, the Joint Task Force is unanimous in its findings. The murder was committed by a person or persons unknown that either did not like guys who passed as girls or did not care for grits. We will continue the investigation until the murderer or murderers are brought to justice."

A local reporter asked, "How long was the list of suspects when you started your investigation?"

Tate answered, "It was the entire population of Guernsey County at the time of the murder. But with our diligent police work, we have narrowed the list down to only ninety-eight as of right now."

MURDER BY MUFFIN

Edna Filbert stretched her bony legs across the leather seat of her luxury tour bus. The ride from Akron to Cambridge was a mere jaunt down Interstate 77, so she still would be fresh and rested upon her arrival at the Ritz-Southgate. Passing vehicles honked at her bus and smiling passengers gave her the "thumbs up" sign. "Fame is grand," she muttered to herself.

The bus was painted school bus yellow and the purple block lettering on the side sported the logo: "LUNCH-LADY CUISINE." Smaller lettering underneath declared: "Go Back to A Simpler Time." The silhouette of a hair-netted woman with a hooked nose adorned the driver's door.

Edna's career in food service began at the tender age of eighteen, when she accepted the position of "salad girl" at the local country club's restaurant. Unfortunately, her slight build brought much unwanted attention. Customers would hand her their doggie bags upon leaving. One gentleman mistakenly thought she was a coat rack and attempted to employ her as such.

The ultimate insult occurred during one Christmas season. A diner who had over-imbibed on champagne noticed Edna in her red and white striped dress. "My word, girl!" he rudely shouted. "With those stripes and that nose, I thought you were a giant candy cane!" Humiliating laughter that seemed to go on for hours echoed around her.

Edna stormed from the restaurant spewing profanities, but at least her dignity was intact; though sadly not for long. Jobs were scarce in those days and Edna was forced to work for a while as a topless waitress in a pancake house.

She finally found her calling as a school cafeteria cook in the Akron city school district. She felt a sense of authority in her white uniform, stockings, and hairnet. If any child showed the slightest hint of disrespect, the mere pointing of her finger banished the pint-sized offender to the principal's office.

For nearly thirty years Edna prepared the dishes that eventually would make her famous: hamburger casserole; macaroni and cheese with baked bread crumbs; meatloaf surprise; and her personal favorite, chili bake with corn muffin. She viewed herself as an artist and government surplus food was her canvas.

When Edna received the news that the school district had contracted with a frozen food company for the school lunches, her heart sank. "I can't work in a restaurant," she lamented. "School food is all I know how to cook." Bingo! If Edna had been a cartoon character, a giant light bulb would have been hovering over her head.

Thus, the idea for *Lunch-Lady Cuisine* was born. Edna knew that her cafeteria-style restaurants would be a hit with baby boomers who longed for the days when school lunches were cooked, not thawed. *The sight of portioned trays and the smell of some form of ground beef cooking could bring on waves of profitable nostalgia*, she reasoned.

Edna was right. Her restaurants in Akron were so successful that she soon opened more in Cleveland, Columbus, and Pittsburgh. After a television appearance on Paula Deen's show, her cafeteria chain went coast-to-coast. Demand for the nostalgic dishes was so great that, on the advice of her business manager, she soon ventured into frozen foods. One could browse the freezer sections of the local Kroger's or Walmart and find "Hot Dog and Cabbage," "Mashed Potatoes with Hamburger Gravy," "Fish Sticks and Carrots," and the vastly popular “Chili Bake with Corn Muffin.” Nearly every freezer in America contained *Lunch-Lady Cuisine* dinners.

As the bus entered the parking lot of the Ritz-Southgate, Edna noticed several law enforcement vehicles. “Must be extra security for the Sheik’s cook-off,” she remarked to her assistant, Teresa.

Edna and Teresa were escorted to their tenth floor suite, where fresh flowers and air fresheners failed to conceal the slight odor of burnt drywall.

“It smells like liver and onions day at the cafeteria,” Edna commented.

“There was a minor incident with the elevator yesterday,” explained the bellhop. “But everything has been taken care of. Enjoy your stay at the Ritz.”

“Teresa,” Edna addressed her assistant. “Start unpacking and draw me a warm bath. I want to go to the kitchen right now to check that all the ingredients for my chili bake are there. After all, I don’t want the Sheik to be disappointed. I should be back in less than ten minutes.”

When thirty minutes elapsed without Edna’s return, Teresa called hotel security.

****POLICE REPORT****

“So, we meet again,” Sheriff McCullum said to Chief Tate as they gathered in the hotel kitchen with officers from both departments. “I don’t know whose jurisdiction this one is, but it doesn’t matter anymore. I understand that the latest victim is Edna Filbert, of *Lunch-Lady Cuisine* fame.”

“Right, Sheriff,” Chief Tate said, looking down at the floor, where the white-dressed sliver of a body lay. “The dent on the left side of her head indicates that some sort of blunt instrument was used.”

Coroner Jane Brickwall kneeled for a closer look at the body. "At least we won't have to scrape her off the wall like that Irishman who was fried in the elevator. Do you see anything in the kitchen that could be the murder weapon?"

Both officers were scanning the room when something yellow caught Sheriff McCullum's eye. "What's this?" he asked as he carefully retrieved the item with his gloved hand. "This was on the floor, behind one of the ovens."

"It looks like a corn muffin," Chief Tate commented.

McCullum observed a speck of blood and some hairnet threads on the muffin. "I've always heard that one of these could kill a buffalo at thirty feet," he remarked while placing the muffin in an evidence bag.

Chief Tate heaved a sigh and leaned against the chrome counter. "Judging by the damage to her temple, I'd say we're looking for a major league pitcher with a blazing fast ball."

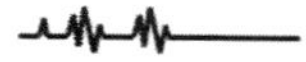

Frostbite Guy Comes to Fry

Scott Shackleton Amundsen-Byrd, the South Pole Station's master chef, wasn't particularly happy to hear birds tweeting, nor to see grass growing in Ohio this year. He'd planned, after all, to be at the Pole by now. The Antarctic was his life! An NSF staff physician and an ill-considered, last-minute Argentinean milkshake had sadly colluded to stop him short of the Pole. He'd flunked the pre-winter physical!

"No sick puppy like you is getting trapped down there on my watch!" declared the obstreperous physician at McMurdo Station's airstrip. The last of the South Pole seasonal shift crew were boarding the plane for their final 800-mile flight southward before night tucked them in for the winter. "I don't care how you think you caught it or how non-contagious you think you are, I can't rule out appendicitis, and I won't have the station smelling like that! Fifty polar Popsicle people can't live on Kaopectate for the next eight months! You're not going! That's final!"

Crusty old Doc Andrews stood beside the Hercules LC-130 aircraft's boarding ramp, staring at "Scotty" with authority, in order to make sure his order was obeyed. In Scotty's mind, the idea of cooking for a spoiled sheik was nowhere on the radar at that dreary moment late on a south polar summer day in February when his world turned upside down. Forced back north until the sun would return, South Pole Station Scotty was locked out of his job, his kitchen, and his continent for all of the winter months to come!

A veteran of more than a dozen previous seasons of dark at the bottom of the world, Chef Amundsen-Byrd had only recently acquired the station nickname "Three-Finger Scotty." It had to do with frostbite. In his first winter as an apprentice chef many years ago, it cost him dearly to take on the philosophy that only sissy girly men refused to play ice football "just because it was cold, windy, and totally dark." Oh, how he mocked the others from his quarterback position on the glacial gridiron! By the time he boarded November's summer relief plane that year, his name had been shortened to "Nine-Finger." Ice football, often played with only a few of the more willing sled dogs, took its toll. Other nicknames followed. He'd been "Four-Finger" just two years back!

Chef Scotty's extreme cryogenic machismo came to him naturally. All four of his great-grandfathers had been legendary Antarctic explorers, as his full name told. Mom's side melded Great-grandpa Roald Amundsen's "first-to-the-South-Pole" drive with Great-grandpa Ernest Shackleton's gritty endurance to watch his exploration ship crushed and sunk by sea ice, only to lead 27 stranded men out of the Antarctic alive. Dad's side provided the pigheaded pluckiness of U.S. Admiral Richard Byrd, who famously (and somewhat pointlessly) sat solo through the winter of 1934 at an inland Antarctic weather station. Further, Dad bequeathed Great-grandpa Robert Falcon Scott's "day-late-and-a-dollar-short" determination to get to the South Pole five weeks after Amundsen, only to freeze to death on his way back. Scotty's breeding was merely an accident of National Geographic Society reunions, which brought together explorer families' offspring just like U.S. Presidents' kids at aircraft carrier christenings. To honor the tradition of his Antarctic ancestors, as if to the manner born, he'd sworn to make a frigid fool of himself ten thousand miles from right-thinking, civilized society—even if it killed him!

Besides ice football, it was frequent icecap hunts for an ancient tent called “Polheim” that cost Scotty dearly in digits. When Great-grandfather Amundsen first erected Polheim a hundred years ago, he thought he’d put it precisely at the South Pole; hence the tent’s name. Careful review of the expedition’s navigational sightings years later revealed that the tent likely lay, however, about a mile and a half from the true geographic pole, the site where Scotty came to be stationed. In what direction? Well, north, of course! There *is* no other direction of travel but north from the South Pole!

Every chance he got, Scotty would grab his divining rods and drag a jackhammer a couple of kilometers “north” of the station, trekking along a different meridian of longitude on each sojourn. His ancestor’s famous Polheim tent had long ago been buried by Antarctic winters’ seasonal snows and now sat impacted in ice—somewhere nearby. No one quite knew where. The divining rods, he always hoped, would lead him to the spot where Great-grandpa Roald left spare equipment and the famous letter addressed to Great-grandpa Robert—the one that broke the poor ‘second-to-the-pole’ man’s heart. Though Scotty never found the tent, at least he’d tried!

The secret weapon in Scotty’s culinary arsenal was a cooking trick he’d learned while experimenting with the cryogenic tanks used to cool sensitive scientific equipment at the station. Liquid nitrogen was in plentiful supply and what started out as a parlor trick—hard-freezing food items like broccoli florets and then shattering them—turned into a gourmand’s delight. The trick was to heat food normally in a skillet and then, with flames still jumping below the pan, pump in liquid nitrogen at -320° Fahrenheit from the top. Shatter with hammer. Refry, and serve. Looked funny. Tasted great!

Cambridge International Cook-off day dawned auspiciously at the Cambridge Ritz-Southgate Hotel as a fresh tank of super-cooled liquid was delivered from ColdStuff-R-Us at New Philadelphia to Scotty in Suite 748. Shortly after the sizzling began, he opened the main tap valve to let the liquid flow in. The instant that coolant hit the pan, however, a sun-like fireball erupted about chef and stove alike. One quick scream and Three-Finger Scotty crumpled to the floor, smoke billowing from his room! Polar chef Scott Shackleton Amundsen-Byrd, freshly flambéed, was dead!

****POLICE REPORT****

Sheriff Mark McCullum arrived at the scene of a fatal room fire at the Cambridge Ritz-Southgate Hotel just as firefighters were preparing to leave. A 37-year-old male chef was found dead. Fire Chief Rudy Blazer explained the fire's origin and nature as follows:

"This guy must have been a flaming idiot! He poured liquid oxygen into a hot skillet over an open fire. No wonder everything exploded! That sort of O_2 concentration can even burn steel."

Upon inspection of the partially charred tank, which Blazer had identified only by shape, size, and color from a distance, McCullum found that the word "Oxygen" was taped over with similar-looking text saying "Nitrogen" in its place. "Does liquid nitrogen explode?" asked McCullum. "No, it puts fires out," came Blazer's reply.

"I think we have a homicide here," declared the sheriff. "Someone wanted this guy dead!"

The resort desk clerk then related a story told to him by the deceased, explaining that he was upset at not being able to serve at the South Pole's scientific station this year.

Suddenly, thinking back to his days in the Wills Creek High School drama club, McCullum exclaimed, "I think I've figured out part of it!" With a mischievous grin, he intoned, "Now is the winter of his discontent, made glorious summer by...well, by a big, flaming ball of oxygen fire! I still have no idea who did it, but at least I've finally found a use for Shakespeare!"

KEYS TO A DISPLEASING FREEZE

Arriving on the Byesville Scenic Railway as if by magic, Hinrik and his elf, Jangles, quietly stepped off the train and hopped on a bicycle for the trip to the Cambridge Ritz-Southgate. Hinrik was the top chef from Iceland and had great plans to win the Cambridge International Cook-off so he could get out of Iceland, where disappointment has always been their main export.

"Isn't this a nice warm place to visit, Jangles? Much warmer than the Ice Cube we came from," said a relaxed, seven-foot-tall Hinrik as they rode up Southgate Parkway. His beautiful Icelandic sweater, made from the special wool of the sheep from home, drew a lot of attention on that hot summer day.

Jangles held on tight while telling Hinrik, "Know what elves like to ride? We like to ride in minivans, just our size." They would be more comfortable too for the dazzling, blonde Jangles in her long gold gown. If only everyone could see her!

Hinrik laughed and said over his shoulder, "If you aren't happy here, you can always go back to Iceland and live under a rock again like the other elves."

Earlier, Hinrik had contacted the Ben Wills Farm to deliver a sheep's head to the Ritz-Southgate so he could prepare that simple dish for the Sheik. Sheep's head is a traditional meat product found in any Icelandic supermarket and very easily prepared. One reason for its great popularity could be the fact that there are two times as many sheep as people on the glacier-covered Iceland. Hinrik definitely hoped that Ben delivered it early so he would have plenty of time to marinate it in the proper spices.

While Hinrik phoned Ben regarding the sheep's head, Jangles went out to collect her favorite thing, keys. What a great place to have some fun! She slipped in and out of resort rooms, easily collecting car keys as she went. Jangles loved music and liked to sing the "Elf-abet." One set of keys she found played the Ohio State fight song, "Across the Field." She placed it in a room occupied by the guy with a Michigan duffle bag. That should annoy him.

From time to time, Jangles took the keys she found back to Hinrik's room. As she mischievously counted the keys in her pile, people raced up and down the halls shouting, "Where are my car keys? I know I left them on the desk."

Jangles giggled, "Oh, what fun!"

Another set of Coca Cola keys was found that played "I'd Like to Teach the World to Sing." Since more Coke is consumed per capita in Iceland than anywhere else in the world, Jangles put them in the room where she saw a Pepsi jacket. Later, she slipped down to the kitchen to get a sandwich, which she insisted be on her favorite bread, "short"bread.

That evening, Hinrik picked up his sheep's head, taking it to his room after singeing the wool off in the BBQ pit outside. Then he scrubbed it clean in a tub under cold water, being especially careful to clean around the eyes and ears. He knew that in order to remove the brain, the easiest way is to freeze it first. So, after the kitchen closed, Hinrik crept down to the Ritz-Southgate kitchen freezer so the brains could freeze quickly. *It shouldn't take too long*, he reasoned.

Once inside, he propped open the door just a little and put the sheep's head way back in the walk-in freezer so it wasn't noticeable. Just then, an orange arm reached in the door and flipped off the light.

Then the freezer door was pushed up tight and "click"—it locked from the outside.

Hinrik didn't know what to do. His cell phone didn't work in the freezer, so he pulled his coat around tightly and hoped that someone would soon come looking for something in the kitchen.

"W-W-Where is J-J-Jangles when you n-n-need her?" stammered a shivering Hinrik.

Early in the morning, the Ritz chef sent his assistant to the freezer to set out some steaks for lunch. When he opened the door, he was shocked to see what appeared to be a frozen Eskimo! Running back into the kitchen, he shouted, "There is a frozen body in the freezer. And it's holding a frosted sheep's head."

****Police Report****

Reports said that another murder victim was found locked in a walk-in freezer at the Ritz-Southgate. Sheriff Mark McCullum remarked, "Appears that there was a double brain freeze going on here: A sheep's brain and a chef's."

Apparently someone noticed a person in an orange jumpsuit shut the freezer door late last night. Witnesses, of course, had no idea there was anyone inside.

Ben Wills was brought in for questioning since he supplied the sheep's head found frozen. Apparently Wills did it for publicity for his farm. "Hinrik told me that when he won the cook-off, he would share the money with me."

"Times are tough on the farm right now," said the old farmer. "The cows are giving powdered milk and the sheep are growing polyester. But I wasn't here when he got locked in the freezer. I was home feeding my sheep."

Outside the door of the freezer, McCullum found the business page from *The Wool Street Journal*. Perhaps someone was perusing it while waiting to be certain that the door remained closed for a while.

"Seems strange that someone from Iceland would get caught in the freezer," said McCullum. "There is a saying in Iceland, "Keep cool with sheep's wool," but I don't think they meant that cool."

Coroner Jane Brickwall said, "The cause of death was from natural causes. It would be perfectly natural to freeze to death if locked in a freezer."

"Bet that chef would rather have been slammed in the Guernsey County jail than in that freezer," remarked one of the deputies.

There was no explanation for the large pile of keys that were found in the frozen chef's room. And they continued to accumulate, even though the chef was long gone. Deputies searched the halls looking for the culprit.

Jangles found a new home at the Ritz-Southgate, away from the cold and isolation of Iceland. Lucky she followed Hinrik on his journey. She was going from room to room singing:

"*Freeze a jolly good fellow,*

Freeze a jolly good fellow..."

She felt quite fortunate that Hinrik led her to the wonderful city of Cambridge.

But was she really responsible for Hinrick's death, or merely someone who was in the right place at the right time?

Peanut Butter and Jelly Sticks to Your Belly

Gliding through the dark night, the black Fokker tri-motor belonging to Harry Jaya kissed the tarmac of Cambridge International Airport shortly after midnight. Taxiing to the end of the runway, the shaded lights of a limo suddenly appeared out of the night and parked by the side entrance.

A tall, gangly figure in a lime green shirt, polka dot pants, and carrying a Pittsburgh Steelers jacket emerged from the side cabin. Several dark shrouded women with parcels on their heads followed quickly and entered the limo. Crouching beside the runway, *Daily Jeffersonian* photographer Mike Mielson captured the entire scene on his Nikon HZL night vision camera. Quickly packing his gear, he jogged to a secluded location adjacent to the Cambridge Ritz-Southgate Hotel.

After parking the limo at the rear entrance of the Ritz-Southgate, Harry was greeted by hotel manager Mitch Metheney. Ducking his head under the doorjamb, Harry paused to speak to the manager.

“I will be preparing a peanut butter, egg, and chocolate jelly soufflé for the Sheik’s breakfast. The entire kitchen must be quarantined for me and my people. The Sheik is an early riser; I will begin my preparations at 5 a.m.”

Pushing the manager aside, Harry skipped down the hall whistling “Three Blind Mice.” He was followed closely by his entourage of dark shrouded native girls.

Turning his cruiser up International Drive to the Ritz-Southgate, Deputy Sheriff Win Chester yawned as he shaded his eyes from the bright lights of the hotel. The flags from the home countries of the chefs in the Cambridge International Cook-off were fluttering in the morning breeze. Pausing briefly at the entrance, Win gazed at the Sheik's huge tent, erected on the front lawn. Across the drive, a herd of camels and goats grazed on the manicured lawn. *All that money,* Win thought, *and this dude camps out in a tent, sleeps on the ground, and rides a camel.*

Crossing the yellow line that divided the hotel jurisdiction between city and county, Win spotted a crumpled figure lying on a bench near the rear entrance. He parked his cruiser next to the bench and walked over to the person, shouting for him to move on. When no reply came, he pulled off the yellow Steelers jacket covering his head. Win stepped back in horror as he discovered the body of a man with his entire head encased in duct tape.

**** POLICE REPORT****

"Get these people out of here!" Sheriff Mark McCullum shouted to Win as he arrived. "This is a crime scene."

Walking up to the bench, McCullum noticed the murder happened just inside the county's jurisdiction. *Well, at least I won't be bothered by Chief Ricky Tate with this one*, he thought as he leaned over to examine the long, lean body.

"Any idea who this clown is, Win? He has to be seven feet tall!"

"No, Mark. All he had on him was a foreign driver's license and a VIP hotel guest key."

"Well, that's a start. Get the coroner down here, and tell the hotel manager I want to talk to him. Now move these people out of here."

Walking back to his cruiser, McCullum was mobbed by reporters covering the cook-off. Holding up his hands, he asked for quiet.

"Now, you people know about as much as I do. When I find out something, you will be the first to know. Just let my people do their work. I'll have a briefing later today."

After meeting with hotel manager Metheney, McCullum called a news conference for four o'clock. As he approached the podium, the sheriff was temporarily blinded by the bright lights of TV cameras from all the major networks.

"Preliminary reports identified the deceased as one Harry Jaya, the chief operating officer of the giant PB&J sandwich chain in Papua, New Guinea. He has an identical twin brother, Dean Jaya, and he was here for the cook-off. Harry checked in a little after midnight and wasn't seen again until his body was discovered just before dawn. Presently, an autopsy is being performed by Coroner Jane Brickwall. The county C.S.I. team is being assisted by Jessica Fletcher from the TV series *Murder, She Wrote*, who is a guest at the hotel."

"Sheriff, what is the PB&J sandwich chain?"

"PB&J stands for peanut butter and jelly. They founded the sandwich chain years ago in New Guinea."

"What do we know about his brother, Dean?" asked a reporter from *USA Today*.

"Harry bought Dean out about ten years ago...I should say forced him to sell his shares. They haven't spoken since. Rumor is Harry feared for his life. That was the reason for his secret arrival."

"Why do they have American names, Sheriff?"

"Their father was a U.S. Marine, Greg. Their mother was a New Guinea native."

Standing up in the back of the room, Chief Ricky Tate from the Cambridge Police Department asked to speak.

"Mark, early this morning my boys arrested a fellow who matches the description of the corpse in the morgue, but he refuses to talk. How do we know who is Harry and who is Dean?"

"Thanks, Ricky, that's a good question. We can talk about that after the autopsy. Now, if there aren't any more questions, I have work to do."

"Just a minute, Mark. I'm not through. That photographer from *The Daily Jeffersonian* gave me a picture taken at three o'clock this morning. It shows the bench where the body was found straddling the city/county line. How do you explain that?"

"I don't know, Ricky, but I'll find out."

"One last thing. If you look closely at this photograph, you will see a tall, slim figure standing in the shadows."

As he walked back to his cruiser, McCullum stopped Deputy Chester.

"How did that photographer get those pictures? I thought we flagged his car? I don't need another jurisdiction battle with the mayor."

"We did, Mark, but he trades vehicles every week and it's hard to keep track of him. Not only that; he is the master of disguise. Remember last year when he dressed up as Bill Clinton and crashed the White House state dinner for the French Premier? He would have gotten away with it if Monica hadn't shown up."

"Well, I want to talk to him. Bring him down to my office, even if you have to arrest him. I want to see what other pictures he has of Harry and his brother."

"Hey, Mark, do you know the difference between an elephant and peanut butter?" Win asked.

"No," McCullum answered impatiently.

"An elephant doesn't stick to the roof of your mouth," the deputy giggled.

Pasta Platter Ticklish Matter

Antonio Gentile gave the bellhop at the gleaming Cambridge Ritz-Southgate a large tip and escorted him unceremoniously from the room. He was extremely nervous. This was his first trip to America and he should have been happy. Leaning against the closed door, he took a deep breath, thinking back on the events of the past few days. Nothing he could put his finger on; it was more a feeling of dread. Was the dark character he'd noticed lurking in the corner of the resort lobby the same person he'd seen several times recently in Italia? Maybe.

Antonio knew he was being tailed. He didn't know by whom, but he was certain he knew why. The burden of carrying around "the secret" weighed heavily on his mental state. Too many family members knew "the secret," the numbers growing with each generation.

Gazing out the window at the cars and huge trucks racing by on Interstate 70, he concluded that there would be no escaping anyone who wanted to do him harm. Should an intruder burst into the room, there was no escape. He looked at the only exit door. The windows were short and skinny, whereas he was tall and fat.

He wasn't sure participating in the Cambridge International Cook-off was such a good idea. Any event that offered millions in prize money was sure to draw many unsavory characters. Antonio's thoughts returned to "the secret," something he'd worried about for years. With today's high-speed communication networking, a criminal could steal and sell "the secret" in a matter of minutes.

Swearing to secrecy at a young age doesn't mean piddlie today, he thought.

Antonio's mind flashed back in time. Years ago, he had the good sense to marry the richest girl in the village, Josephina, the daughter of ristorante owner Louis Maracella. She was ugly as sin, and sometimes referred to by the boys on the village square as Jo-Jo, the dog-faced girl. But she had one redeeming quality. Along with her money came the secret to her family's vast fortune, whispered to him during a romantic interlude.

Antonio was shocked to learn that the famous marinara served by her father at his ristorante was none other than Chef Boyardee, repackaged and relabeled. The secret was the spaghetti itself, homegrown on the family farm located near the village and the Gentile ristorante, where the large sign in front read "Servire le Teste Incoronate di Europa!" *(Serving the Crowned Heads of Europe!)*

Row after row of lovingly tended spaghetti trees covered the rolling hills. Antonio thought that this would be a good year to enter a contest calling for a very easily prepared down-home dish. He was sure he had just the ticket. If the Sheik wanted simple, he'd give him simple.

The weather had been superb. Gentle rains in the spring; warm nights when you could almost hear the trees blossoming, the Italian sunshine warming the earth, and this year, for a change, no labor problems. The ladders and drying racks had been repaired by a few of the family members who lived on the spaghetti farm year-round, while others of the group worked at the Gentile ristorante.

Antonio's thoughts again turned to the identity of the person who might want to harm him. First on the list was Franco, that sneaky-eyed, lazy, good-for-nothing brother-in-law. No love lost there. Franco had always been jealous of Antonio. Josephina's father had become quite fond of his son-in-law and made him and Josephina his heirs, knowing his son to be a lowdown rotten jerk.

Yes, Franco, now without status or fortune, had plenty of reason to want his sister's husband out of the way. But wait...what about that greasy, long-haired kid with the lopsided grin who had been hanging around his daughter, Sophia? What would he have to gain? Sophia and money, that's what. The prizes for winning this contest would be enough for some to commit murder.

And then there's Palo DeNiro. He has been lurking around the restaurant a lot lately.

Antonio was a little on the plump side and very tall. He had thick eyebrows over mischievous brown eyes. A large, well-groomed mustache only partially hid pearly white teeth. He was rather handsome in a curious way and was also something of a ladies' man. Nothing serious; mostly just little flirtations. But lately these had included Palo's wife, Rosa, the pasticceria chef. The woman was a black-eyed curvaceous woman who was not above flaunting her many charms for any and all to admire. There was something about the way she rolled out a pie crust that made his heart skip a beat.

Antonio hadn't admitted it to himself but he was beginning to have designs on the woman. Only his love for Josephina had prevented him from making a terrible mistake. That, and his great fear of her. He did not wish to encounter her wrath, for he knew she wouldn't hesitate to hit him over the head with a flatiron. His wife was very strong and not at all backward.

Yes, I must consider Palo. He's a suspicious man and, after all, we once competed for the hand of ugly, but very rich, Josephina.

Tilly, the maid, let herself into Suite 608 at about nine-thirty that evening. She would turn down the bed, freshen the bathroom linens and place a gorgeous orchid and several imported chocolates on the pillow.

Entering the bedroom, she was startled to see the occupant stretched out on the chaise lounge. Mr. Gentile was fully clothed, except that his shoes and socks had been removed. Duct tape around his wrists and ankles held him securely to the chair. Not that he was going anywhere. Mr. Gentile was now the late Mr. Gentile and dead as the proverbial doornail. “Too bad,” Tilly shrugged, dialing 911.

****POLICE REPORT****

Tilly flipped on the TV, waiting for the police to arrive. *What’s keeping those clowns?* she wondered. *I’d like to get out of here. I still have four more suites to do.* She lit a cigarette and took a couple of swallows from an open wine bottle on the table. *Not bad*, she smiled to herself.

Just then the law arrived, wearing immaculately pressed uniforms and shiny badges. They introduced themselves to Tilly, who gave them a curt nod then returned to the “Law and Order” rerun.

The officers noted Tilly’s lack of emotion at finding the dead guest. Still, this was the third body she’d discovered this week. You can get used to anything.

The officers turned to the deceased, looking for bullet holes, knife wounds, anything that might explain the cause of death. Other than a wide-open mouth containing a small garlicky meatball, they saw nothing unusual.

Carefully inspecting the soles of the man’s bare feet, Sheriff Mark McCullum turned to Police Chief Ricky Tate and dramatically announced, “This man has been tickled to death. Definitely murder. Call the coroner.”

Tate nodded. “That meatball could have used a little more oregano,” he said solemnly.

Going Green Can Be Obscene

Matilda Alambee Bakana, popular Aboriginal chef, jumped at the chance to compete in the Cambridge International Cook-off for several reasons. First, it might give her a chance to meet the dream love of her life, the Reverend Al Sharpton. Second, she was in trouble for illegally raising Tasmanian devils and komodo dragons in a state-owned penguin rookery near her farm.

Prominent Australian and New Zealanders were willing to pay a high price for trained Tasmanian devils and komodo dragons to guard their gated estates. It was a prestige thing, nothing more, although the almost-prehistoric creatures were extremely vicious.

What law enforcement didn't know was that Matilda also headed a lucrative exotic bird smuggling operation. Monthly, she exported hundreds of rare birds—namely the short-tailed shearwater and the sooty oystercatcher—to pet stores across the United States.

Author of the popular cookbook "What to Do With a Kangaroo," Matilda lived on an atoll between the Christmas and New Year Islands in Tasmania, off Australia's southwest coast.

In her corner of the world, she was renowned for her eel-tailed catfish stuffed with turtle eggs, yams, and red beets, then wrapped in a crocodile bladder and tossed on hot coals. *But that's too exotic for the Cambridge simple food contest*, she reflected. She'd have to lighten up her meal. *The Sheik wants only simple food.*

Because she'd never worn shoes, Matilda had size eighteen webbed feet. She was the fastest swimmer on the Australian Olympic Swim Team but was ruled ineligible for competition because officials said her huge feet gave her an unfair flipper advantage.

While she served kangaroo meat that tasted like top grade beef, Matilda owned a large chain of outdoor food stands in several countries in the Southern Hemisphere. Her specialty was balut eggs, fertilized duck eggs with nearly-developed embryos inside that are boiled and eaten in the shell.

Business people in the downtown areas of cities like Tokyo and Sydney regularly took time out during their busy day to down a couple of balut eggs as mid-morning or mid-afternoon pick-me-ups. Popularly believed to be an aphrodisiac and considered a high-protein, hearty snack, baluts were mostly sold by Matilda's several hundred licensed street vendors.

For three days prior to leaving Tasmania for Cambridge, Matilda got on her computer and studied every aspect of Guernsey County, Ohio. She was particularly interested in the fish, frogs, turtles, crawdads, salamanders, and mussels found in Wills Creek. *Perfect*, she mused. *Plus,* she surmised, *the people who live in that area appear to be a friendly lot, unlike many of the Aussies and Kiwis I often have to deal with.*

Instead of packing a lot of foods from her native land, Matilda decided to prepare a simple meal made entirely of things she could find in the creek that ran through Cambridge. She ignored the research material relating to the creek water's questionable purity. No matter that studies showed the cloudy water contained several unhealthy contaminants. After all, she reasoned, she grew up in the Tasmanian bush where all the water was brown, kept that way by the giant crocodiles that inhabited those rivers. There were no crocodiles in Wills Creek; surely the water would be much safer than what she'd been drinking for thirty-five years.

Staffers at the Cambridge Ritz-Southgate could only stare when Matilda entered the lobby to register. Standing six feet tall, she weighed just over a hundred pounds. Her heavily creased, leathery face was the color of extremely dark, overripe plums. Her coarse black hair stood straight up and her nose was flatter than Mike Tyson's punching bag. Resort personnel, however, were impressed when her friendly pet koala bear rolled over, played dead, and shook hands with guests in the lobby.

At nightfall, Matilda took a flashlight and some other equipment and, sitting on a large metal serving tray, slid down the hill to Wills Creek. There, she quickly speared a large carp, several frogs and salamanders, a small turtle, and a dozen crawdads. Climbing back up the hill, she slipped into one of the resort's deserted kitchens and set about experimenting with a seafood chowder made entirely of ingredients she'd taken from Wills Creek.

The breakfast chef got the shock of his life when he reported for work the next morning. He didn't have to flip on the kitchen lights to see the lump that was spread-eagled and tied to the counter. Matilda was dead all right, her body emitting a bright green glow that lit up the entire kitchen. A lime-colored foam covered the bottom of her face.

****POLICE REPORT****

Sheriff Mark McCullum picked up Dr. Jane Brickwall, the coroner, and sped to the Cambridge Ritz-Southgate. It was not yet daylight. He knew that a corpse that glowed in the dark would require some intense investigation from someone with a medical background. "Something fishy going on here," he told deputies.

Inside the kitchen door was a pair of hip boots with the toes cut out to accommodate size eighteen feet, a frog gig, and a large net. Outside, deputies found wet footprints leading up the hill from Wills Creek to the rear hotel door.

"Someone stuck a bunch of fish and frogs and salamanders and crawdads into her mouth and forced this woman to eat them," Dr. Brickwall said. Her face twisted as if she might vomit herself.

"But how could that kill her?" the sheriff asked.

"It wasn't the seafood itself," Dr. Brickwall opined thoughtfully. "It was the creek water. Apparently, it's so polluted that it's now fatally toxic."

"It's ghastly the way the green fluorescence lights up the body like a Christmas tree."

"Well, it certainly proves that Kermit the Frog was right when he sang 'It's not easy being green...'" Dr. Brickwall smiled tightly.

"Someone else who talks a lot about green is Al Gore," McCullum mused. "I'll give him a call."

KRAUT PACKS A LOT OF CLOUT

Ramrod-straight, Konrad von Knödelmeister strutted purposefully into the kitchen of the Cambridge Ritz-Southgate. The barrel-chested, mustachioed Küchenchef from Kaiserslautern, Germany, barked orders while his apprentices, Timm and Luka, cringed.

"I *vill* have alles in Ordnung!" Adjusting his monocle, he peered closely at his errant charges, releasing a frustrated moan. "Luka, ist das ein fresh apron, already mit curry sauce beschmiert? Ach, du liebe! I am plagued mit incompetents!" He glared at the two indignantly. With one last loud huff, he clicked his heels military-style, did an about-face, shoved through the double doors, and marched down the hallway.

"He'll be in a better mood after his massage," Timm whispered to Luka encouragingly. "Schöne mädchen *(pretty girls)* alvays make him happy."

"I'm chust glad he vasn't carrying his riding crop today," sighed Luka with relief.

Twenty minutes later, wearing only a towel, his monocle, and a broad smile, Konrad eased his considerable bulk onto a warm massage table. Jacqui Hanzon, the owner of the day spa on Woodlawn Avenue, stepped into the room wearing a flowered turquoise sarong.

"I'll be your masseuse today, Herr Knodelmeister," she smiled. Sleek and tanned, she pulled her long dark hair back into a loose bun, with Konrad studying her every move. Wisps of her hair framed the face of an angel. Konrad thought, *Could this be Heaven?*

"Are you ready for your massage, Herr Knödelmeister?" The words dripped from her lips like honey. Konrad only drooled. Jacqui cast her eyes skyward in a "why me?" expression as she assessed the magnitude of the job before her. The aroma of coconut oil cut delicately into Konrad's musings as she anointed her hands and began kneading his thick neck. After a few heady minutes of massage, Konrad loosened up nicely. She asked sweetly, "Feel good, Herr Knödelmeister?"

"Wunderbar! You haf sehr gut hands, mein Schatz," he ventured warily. "Perhaps I could entice you…"

She interrupted sharply. "My name, Herr Knödelmeister, is Jacqui." With an unexpected strength that made him wince, she pummeled his broad shoulders with forceful authority. *Some days, my black belt in karate and all those years in the LPWA (Ladies Professional Wrestling Association) really pay off*, she thought to herself. To Konrad, she cooed, "You're really tight today. Let me work the stiffness out of those muscles." She proceeded to dish out a torturously rigorous massage, hitting all the pressure points with impunity. Konrad discovered, much to his heightening angst, that his angel had a bit of a mean streak. He could do no more than manage an occasional pained whimper.

When the massage was over, Konrad felt more like Der Wet Knödel than Der Knödelmeister. Jacqui smiled with satisfaction as he slid limply from the table, murmuring a repentant "Danke schön, Jacqui." Submissively backing out the door with one hand holding the towel around his vast middle and the other fumbling with his monocle, he found himself wishing he'd visited Kennedy's Bakery instead.

Back at the hotel, after a recuperative hot shower and a double Schnapps for a severely bruised ego, Konrad's spirits lifted considerably. He donned a shepherd shirt and his lederhosen then headed for the hotel kitchen. Timm and Luka were busily finishing their assigned culinary tasks.

Konrad stiffly assessed their work, pronouncing it "Sehr gut!" with a wide grin. His apprentices surreptitiously exchanged knowing looks.

As Konrad collected ingredients for the main course, he sang lustily, his rich tenor voice echoing throughout the hotel. He loved singing the alte Deutsche Lieder *(old German songs)*.

Crowning his signature bratwurst reuben sandwiches with sauerkraut, red onion, scallion, and green pepper, he yodeled, "Du! Du! Liegst mir im Herzen, du, du, liegt mir im Sinn…," *(You, you, are always in my heart; you, you are always on my mind)*. His apprentices struggled to conceal the pained expressions on their faces.

Luka plated sandwich halves on Bitburger Pils luncheon plates, brought along especially for the occasion, while Timm drew frothy steins of the master's favorite draught. The steamy, vinegary smell of sauerkraut permeated the air, drawing a tear to the eye.

Adjusting his monocle, Konrad did a Schottisch across the lineoleum to check the pommes frites *(French fries)*. "Gut! Alles fertig! *(All done!)* Timm, komm hier bitte!"

While Timm plated pommes frites, Konrad added finishing touches to the Zitronenküchen, a "wunderbar" lemon cake, for the dessert finale.

"Gut!" He grinned excitedly at his apprentices. "You go now. I vill komm ven der Sheik summons." Timm and Luka quickly wheeled their serving carts to the dining room.

"Ja, ja, ja, ja, weisst nicht wie gut ich dir bin," *(Yes, yes, yes, yes, you don't know how good I am [for you])* Konrad trilled jubilantly. He polkaed lightly around the prep island, pausing briefly to enjoy the bouquet of the steaming sauerkraut.

The tersely whispered "Nein, nein, nein, NEIN," registered only vaguely as he futilely resisted the strong hands that forced his head into the simmering vat. Three minutes later, Konrad's polka was pretty much pickled.

**** POLICE REPORT ****

Sauerkraut juices puddled around the deceased body of Chef Konrad Knödelmeister. The coroner, Dr. Jane Brickwall, stood in the far corner with a hankie over her nose, eyes watering from the stench of spilled sauerkraut.

This job really stinks, sniffed Sheriff Mark McCullum as he wrote furiously in a small wire-bound notebook. The clattering of the falling pot of fermented cabbage had brought the chef's apprentices racing to the kitchen, but efforts to resuscitate the sauerkraut-covered chef were futile. The sheriff had sent the two distraught German youths to the dining room with a deputy to await further questioning. He watched them leave carrying a couple steins of Bitburger Pils and knew they'd soon feel much better. Truth be told, he would have liked to join them.

The sheriff joined the coroner as she opened a window to let in some air. "Well, Jane, what do you make of this mess?" he asked.

"Hmm. From the amount of sauerkraut in his mouth and up his nose," she answered thoughtfully, "I'd have to guess he was stewed in his own juices. I'll let you know if we find anything different, but I'm pretty confident on this one, Mark."

Sauerkraut everywhere, incapacitated surveillance cameras, and wet tracks from a man's size 8 shoe leading through the doors and down the hall—that's all we've got to go on, the sheriff reviewed mentally, gritting his teeth in frustration. *The killer simply vanishes into thin air like steam over the sauerkraut pot—again. This guy's modus operandi sure leaves a bad taste in your mouth.*

Rub-a-Dub-Dub, Dead Man in the Tub

Zeke Holcomb looked like someone who had escaped from the Hee Haw TV show when he checked into the Cambridge Ritz-Southgate Hotel. He was dressed in a pair of faded blue bib overalls, a wrinkled #3 Dale Earnhart sweatshirt, ankle-high lace up brogan shoes, and a slightly ragged straw hat.

Cambridge was not all that far from Booger Holler, West Virginia, in miles, but it was far removed in time. Zeke's head was filled to the very top with visions of fame and fortune. He had been told about the Sheik's Cambridge International Cook-off by Bobbi Jo Wiggens, the seventeen-year-old dayshift waitress at Bubba's Drive-In and Carryout where they both worked. She had read about it in the *Charleston Gazette* a customer had left at a booth.

Zeke had to get one of the cook-off committee persons to help him with the registration because his reading and writing skills were a little rusty. His signature dish, barbequed buzzard gizzards with chitterlings, drew more than a few snickers from the large group of reporters covering the sign-in booth. Zeke made up his mind to ignore the rowdy group. They were probably just bunch of ignorant Yankees, anyway.

The bellhop assigned to show Zeke to his room had to explain the workings of all those modern contraptions like indoor plumbing, electric lights, telephone, and television to the young man from the hills. After tipping the bellhop a whole quarter, Zeke stood in the middle of the room and marveled at all the new things he had just learned.

First things first, as Granny used to say, he thought as he began unpacking his new Sunday-go-to-meeting bib overalls and best flannel shirt. He had worn his everyday bibs and best sweatshirt to travel in. Zeke figured some of the wrinkles inherent in the nearly new denim bibs would come out if they were hung up overnight behind the cook stove. But he could not find any stove in his room. *Well, them britches ain't all that wrinkly.*

Zeke sat in one of the plush chairs and thought about the cook-off. He didn't have any doubts about winning it. After all, he had been cooking for five years at Bubba's, and before that he had been the breakfast cook for two whole years at the Huddle House in Bluefield, West Virginia. He had even lasted two whole weeks at a Waffle House and that was a darn sight more than most could say.

Besides, it was not really his fault a boneheaded deputy sheriff had to get his underwear in an uproar because a couple of breakfast orders got mixed up. But Deputy Dawg had got mouthy and Zeke had whacked him over the head with a cast-iron skillet. That little whack cost him thirty days swinging a brush hook for the county and his job at Waffle House.

Zeke figured he was going into this cook-off with a slight handicap; this rule about no pork would be difficult to overcome. It was just second nature for a country boy to use some part of a hog in every dish. He supposed he could use deer chitterlings, but it just would not be the same thing.

How could those people survive without eating hog meat? Maybe he would just lie about using the deer chitterlings and use pork anyway. That ol' Sheik probably wouldn't know the difference. The Sheik might just change his mind about pig meat after eating some of Zeke's cooking.

He went down to the lobby and asked the clerk to place a phone call to his cousin, Sim Basket. Momma had told him Sim lived somewheres close around Cambridge. When he had Sim on the phone, Zeke asked him where he could find fresh deer and hog chitterlings hereabouts. Sim promised he would be glad to take care of that little chore for a family member.

Cooking the gizzards and chitterlings in his homemade sauce until they were tender was only the first step. His side dish of road-killed opossum combined with a green bean casserole was good enough to make your mouth water. A generous slice of sweet potato and pawpaw pie liberally doused with white lightening would literally set your taste buds aflame. Yep, he was ready to cook.

Zeke smiled at the thought of all that prize money. The only palace he had ever heard of was the Palace Theater in downtown Bluefield. He wouldn't have any use for them fancy limos. They were much too long to make it all the way up Booger Hollow Road. Maybe the Sheik would let him trade the limo in on a new Chevy 4x4. Zeke had a feeling there must be something wrong with the fourteen year-old girls if the Sheik was giving them away. Most girls that age already had a husband and a baby or two.

****POLICE REPORT****

Zeke Holcomb's body was discovered when maintenance workers entered his room to find out why water was leaking into the room below. They found his nude body floating face down in the still overflowing bathtub. They immediately turned off the faucet and pulled the body from the tub to the bathroom floor. Two men began giving Zeke artificial respiration while a third man called 9-1-1.

The emergency medical technicians arrived within minutes and took over for the maintenance men, but it was too late to save the victim. Sheriff Mark McCullum, Cambridge Police Chief Ricky Tate, and Guernsey County Coroner Jane Brickwall all arrived at the same time. Brickwall examined the body briefly and declared the preliminary cause of death was drowning, but she could not determine if it was murder or accidental before a complete autopsy.

McCullum and Tate each tried to say the body was found in the other's jurisdiction. This was a frequent matter of discussion, since the line between the county and the city ran directly through the middle of the hotel.

McCullum said, "Now, Tate, you know danged well it's your turn. I took the heat for the last murder in the hotel and we agreed from the beginning that we would take turn about. So just quit whining and get on with the investigation."

Tate replied, "No, what we agreed on was to take turn about *if* we could not determine exactly whose jurisdiction was involved. This crime scene is plainly in the county. The city line does not start until you get just beyond that corner down the hall."

The sheriff heatedly replied, "No, sir. We agreed that when this hotel was involved we would take turns and it is your turn. Just quit trying to weasel out of the deal and get on with the investigation."

Tate replied, "Maybe the murder was committed in the county and the body moved into the city limits. I'm going to have to check in with the Mayor on this one."

Beauty Falls for Sheik

Pilar Alvarez stood in the bathroom of the luxurious suite on the fourth floor of the Ritz-Southgate. As she loosely tied the sash on her floral satin pajamas, she gazed at her image in the wall-sized mirror.

"Qué bonita," she said in self-adoration. Her tall, shapely form had earned her the first runner up position in the Miss Peru beauty contest four years earlier. She would have won, Pilar told herself, if the winner's father had not been a hot-shot politico.

Her exotic good looks resulted from the chromosomal combination of an Incan mother and a Thai father. As a child, Pilar endured frequent teasing about her almond-shaped eyes and lanky legs, but the venture into puberty turned the teasing into near-constant admiration of her unique beauty. Her hometown of Cusco provided many opportunities for her to showcase her natural gifts. She was invited to grand openings of new businesses; she served as "queen" or "princess" at parades; she presented trophies at sporting events. She was available for any event that needed a smiling, hand-waving beauty queen.

However, Pilar's most important role was with the Inti Raymi festival that took place every June. The festival, based on an ancient Inca celebration of the sun god, was the second largest in all of South America. Hundreds of thousands of people from every part of the world would flock to Cusco to enjoy the festivities. Parades, fireworks, music, and good food made Inti Raymi the Mardi Gras of the southern hemisphere.

Every year for Inti Raymi, Pilar and her mother would make a huge pot of cuy chactado to sell in the food court. The dish, a mainstay in most Peruvian homes, consisted of fried guinea pigs with peppers and onions. Pilar and her mother added potatoes and secret seasonings to their cuy chactado, making it the most popular food at the festival.

On what was to be her lucky day, Pilar served a distinguished-looking man a bowl of her famous dish. She also gave him a wink and a smile. He was Jorge Hernandez, a television executive from Lima. Within a month Pilar had her own cooking show, *La Cocina de Pilar*, which soon became the most popular show on Spanish-speaking television. As Pilar prepared chicken and rice or chinchilla and beans, she made certain that the camera also caught her low-cut designer blouse and her long legs in Tony Lama boots. Soon her picture graced the covers of fashion magazines as well as those for cooking enthusiasts.

Pilar became the most sought-after talk show guest in South America. She loved tossing her shining black hair over her shoulder while flashing her toothpaste-commercial perfect smile at the camera. She imbued the most mundane kitchen tasks with sensuality. *Cosmopolitan* magazine placed her picture on the cover of the December issue, which became their most popular cover ever. She posed cross-legged under the mistletoe, wearing a Santa hat and a garment that was little more than a scarf. The caption read: “See What Pilar Is Cooking Up for the Holidays!” A life-size poster of the cover was in the locker room of the New York Jets, according to various sports writers.

Still admiring her image in the mirror, Pilar’s thoughts turned to the Sheik. At the age of twenty-three, she knew that she was the youngest chef in the competition and was certain that she was also the most beautiful. Without the Sheik’s knowledge, Pilar had arranged an “accidental” private meeting with him the next morning.

She would wear her aqua Dior dress that accented her twenty-four-inch waist and use her best catwalk strut to impress him. He would be putty in her hands when she finished.

As Pilar prepared for bed, she unpacked a contraption that had been her night-time companion since the age of ten: a restraint that buckled around the waist and attached to the bed frame. Pilar was a somnambulist, more commonly known as a sleepwalker. After securing herself in the safety device, she closed her eyes and drifted off to sleep.

She did not hear the door squeak open as a dark figure entered the room, nor did she hear the sliding glass door to the balcony open. However, her subconscious did hear, "Get up, Pilar! You have a zit on your nose—a big, ugly, pus-filled zit! You must pop it before the Sheik sees you!"

Pilar heard the click of the restraint's belt, but did not awaken. With her hand grabbing at her nose, she arose from the bed.

"This way!" someone whispered while guiding her toward the balcony. "You must climb this step before getting to the mirror." With her eyes still closed, Pilar climbed over the railing and plunged four floors to a cold, muddy death in Wills Creek.

****POLICE REPORT****

Sheriff McCullum stood on the creek bank with Coroner Brickwall as the body of Pilar Alvarez was loaded into the ambulance.

"What a shame," commented Dr. Brickwall. "This girl had everything going for her. I don't believe that it's suicide."

"Neither do I, with all the other killings going on," remarked McCullum. "Chief Tate, let's take a look at her room."

The sheriff's eyes nearly popped from his head when he saw the restraint on the bed. "Someone was torturing the poor girl!" he blurted.

"No, Sheriff," Tate said. "That's a restraint to keep sleepwalkers in bed at night. I know, because my younger brother used to sleepwalk as a kid. He'd wander all over the house gathering trash baskets and then dump them into the toilet. He couldn't remember any of it the next morning. After some huge plumbing bills, Dad finally got a belt like this for him. It worked like a charm."

"So the beauty was a sleepwalker," McCullum said, gently fingering a crucifix on the nightstand. "She must have been a roamin' Catholic."

Chernobyl Goes Mobile

"You gotta concrete room in basement?" asked the heavyset Polynesian chef leaning on the Cambridge Ritz-Southgate Hotel's registration desk. The desk clerk looked puzzled. "I gotta me my oven. Lotsa lead. Real heavy. See?" Chef Kriti Kamas Gub-Ang pointed to the flatbed truck parked outside the lobby's glass doors.

Strapped to its platform was a mysterious slate gray object the shape and size of a small refrigerator. Chef Gub-Ang glowed with pride as he waved toward the strange gray thing.

The strange gray thing glowed, too.

"Pardon me, sir. Did I hear you correctly that you would like a room in the basement?" replied Matilda, the startled clerk.

"Yes, you betcha! Lotsa concrete on floor! You got concrete ceilings, too? Hope so. Cinderblocks? No need window. Gotta cook. Cook! Cook! Cook! Keep evy-body safe! Whole hotel safe! So... you got room in basement?"

Safe!? Matilda had become accustomed to strange, quirky chefs in the recent days of contestant check-ins, but this was the first one to fret about public danger as he waddled in the door. And what was up with concrete in the basement?

"I'm sorry, sir, but we don't have any guest rooms in the basement. There's a suite available on the second floor above the Bigfoot Ballroom. Would that suit your purpose?"

"No, no, no! Gotta cook in da basement. Special problem. Oven so heavy. Weigh like hundred tuna fish. You get manager. He say 'Okey Dokey Dominokey.' Gotta go room in basement chop-chop!"

It took thirty minutes and interventions at two levels of hotel management to grant the troubled chef his wish. Fortunately, head janitor Les Kleen solved the problem with a call to Reg Barnert, proprietor of local Barnert Paper Supply. "Can you push back delivery on that next special order truckload of brokerage-scented Mogul-Wipe toilet paper for about three days? We got a nut job checkin' in. Wants to camp out in the storage room. Says he loves bein' around concrete!" Buoyant, balding Reg was glad to oblige.

Chef Gub-Ang hailed from the Marshall Islands, halfway between Hawaii and Australia, in the middle of the Pacific Ocean. More specifically, gray-haired Gub-Ang was born on the Marshalls' Bikini Atoll in late 1945, only to be relocated within days, along with his family, to nearby Kili Island, making way for the 1946 atomic bomb tests at Bikini. Awed by the might of U.S. weaponry, the chef-to-be's parents named him for the giant power being brought to Bikini by the Americans—as best they understood it. With a brave new name like Kriti Kamas Gub-Ang, he would surely go far in the brave new nuclear world!

As a child, Chef Gub-Ang grew up with one foot in his native South Sea world of pineapples and catamarans and the other foot in the world of military nuclear scientists at the Kili base.

On base, young Kriti learned to cook. Senior scientist Arnie Benedict took the lad under his wing and showed him the secrets of the "magic cooking rocks." The "magic" rocks were really just two heavy metallic lumps. Individually, they were unremarkable. But, put them within a foot of each other, and they'd heat up like crazy!

"Promise me, Kriti, that you will never let the magic rocks touch each other without my permission. That would stop the magic," Arnie counseled. "In fact, keep them in a thick lead oven!" Kriti dutifully complied.

As Kriti grew to manhood, his fellow former-Bikini relatives came to cherish his skills with the magic cooking rocks. Since Kili

Island had no lagoon, their usual diet of spear-caught, shallow water sea life had vanished! Neither were the coconut trees of Kili sufficient to support its newfound population. One day, the U.S. government sent a concerned anthropologist to the island, along with a boatload of shiny silver cylinders for its residents. The scientist also brought strange silver sticks. “These, my friends, are can openers,” he explained. “Learn how to use ’em. It’s time you started eating like Americans! In thirty years, we’ll send a cardiologist.”

Unfortunately, eating American was not what the islanders had in mind. Spam and applesauce just didn’t taste anything like freshly caught flounder from the old lagoon. That’s where Kriti came in. He and his magic cooking rocks went on to reinvent South Sea cuisine! His hut became a diner. Within years, it became a dynasty.

Unto Kili’s prestigious Marshall Island Manor, the rich and the powerful flocked for the Chef Gub-Ang “experience.” No matter their tastes or preferences going in, not a patron left his luau who was not glowing. Was it all about the food? Not really. Kriti’s radiant personality? Perhaps. Or the mysterious scintillations in Chef Gub-Ang’s sparkling eyes? Mesmerizing! The magic rocks held close their secret.

As the Guernsey County Courthouse clock tolled twice through the clear night air, muffled footsteps slowed and stopped outside the door of Ritz-Southgate basement storeroom TP-1. The Post-It note pushed under the door was not discovered by Chef Gub-Ang until he rose at five. Upon reading it, Kriti waddled to the oven and reached inside. With a sharp report and sudden flash of intense blue light, a sizzling sound and steam erupted, first from the oven, and then from the floor beneath. Chef Gub-Ang staggered backwards, falling. Before help could arrive, Chef Kriti Kamas Gub-Ang was dead!

**** POLICE REPORT ****

Responding to a five-seventeen a.m. alarm at the Cambridge Ritz-Southgate, Sheriff Mark McCullum literally smelled danger. Blessed with the nose of a sniffer dog, McCullum instantly picked up the pungent scent of nuclear fallout! Racing against time, he confirmed one dead lei-clad chef and peered quickly into the deep, red-hot hole in the floor beside the body. Dashing from the toxic room, he padlocked its steel door behind him.

"Everyone out of the basement!" screamed McCullum at the top of his lungs. "Bozo here just melted down his nuclear reactor! It's the China Syndrome!"

After clearing and ventilating the basement level, McCullum briefed resort management on the situation. "I've got some good news and some bad news for you. The good news is that the concrete walls and floors here make decent radiation shields. The bad news is you've got a brand new Chernobyl Room downstairs. You're gonna have to find somewhere else to store your toilet paper. Keep that room sealed off for a while."

"How long?" asked the day shift manager.

"Oh, ten or twenty thousand years should do it," McCullum replied, absentmindedly pulling a sticky note off his shoe. "Hmmm... this note says, 'HOT NEW RECIPE: Touch rocks together for taste of heaven.—Yours truly, Arnie!'" McCullum's brow furrowed. "You know, if those 'rocks' were enriched uranium, they probably reached critical mass on contact. This note means it was murder! We're lucky those 'rocks' didn't blow Guernsey County sky high!! Hey, what did you say that guy's name was?"

"Kriti Kamas Gub-Ang."

"Sounds a lot like 'Critical Mass Go Bang' to me," mused McCullum. "What an ironic name! I wonder how he got it."

Whipped By a Ripped Chip

Rolling from her private jet at Cambridge International Airport, Anne Marie Gableton was as round as she was tall. Her braided red hair made a fiery entrance as she carried her special recipes in a mint green handbag filled with Prince Edward Island potatoes. Headed to the Cambridge Ritz-Southgate, this famous chef was dressed in a long, green dress that made her resemble the roundest leprechaun imaginable.

Prince Edward Island had been home to this fireball all her life. She was the victor in the Humpty Dumpty Cook-off nearly every year. Her Creamy Meadow Mouse Gnocchi, made with freshly trapped organic mice, had been served during the Queen's visit. Her Majesty especially enjoyed the refreshing, cold tea served with "mice cubes."

Arriving in Cambridge to win the $10 million Cambridge International Cook-off prize, Anne Marie planned to build a large statue of a potato on Prince Edward Island and also eliminate all the cats on the island. She didn't like cats as they ate her birds--all of them! First, it was the mice that caused the problem. She remembered as a little girl how she used to spear mice with a pitchfork in their potato barn. Imported cats finished off the mice, but then the cats began eating all the birds. Then the island was overrun by cats. What confusion in the old food chain! But Annie hoped that soon she would be "in the chips" with her big prize win.

"Good potato chips taste like Conn's" was a slogan she had heard all the way up to Prince Edward Island, where the thin and crispy

Anne of Green Gables were the favorite chips. Her first stop was J&T's Market at Derwent, where she talked to Tim, the owner. He was also one of the owners of Conn's Potato Chips, so his market had the freshest chips around. Tim told his drivers, "You have to handle those bags of chips as gently as you would a baby. No one likes crumpled chips."

At the market, Tim greeted Anne Marie. "Welcome to Guernsey County. Yer a fer piece down the road."

"Comment ca flippe," Anne Marie responded with their traditional Arcadian French greeting. "I came all this way just to taste your famous Conn's Potato Chips."

"These were made fresh this morning. Sometimes the chips might ask each other: Should we go for a dip?"

"Silly! Mmm…this tastes like a potato chip should taste. Have you ever tried dipping them in chocolate?" asked Anne before leaving the store. "That is a favorite back home."

Eventually, checking into her room at the Ritz-Southgate, she discovered a cat outside her door. Before she left the island, the Premier told her, "Be nice to their cats. Some of those people in the United States actually keep them for pets. Cat hair in their food is just considered extra fiber. Why, some of them even call home to talk to their cats!"

She proceeded to take out her boot gun, hidden under her long skirt, and fired it into the air to scare the cat down the hallway instead of finishing it off. No one paid any attention to gunshots at the Ritz, as this had been heard often when the drug cartel visited town.

Anne Marie's intention was to serve the best fish and chips the Sheik had ever eaten. PEI Cat Strips & Chips were sold at roadside stands all around Prince Edward Island and were easily made. First, she needed to locate the best fresh fish locally, as she couldn't use cat strips here! *Bet those guys in the parking lot with the inflatable boat named "She Got the House" in the back of their pickup would have a good idea where to get fresh fish*, she thought.

After talking with them, they said, "Shur'nuff, we can git yuens all the fish you want. Tell us when to bring it to y'all and we'll do it. We'll go to Salt Fork Lake and catch 'em early in the morning.'"

While reading *101 Things to Do with a Potato*, Anne Marie drifted off to sleep peacefully with her cook-off plans complete. Dreams of mashed potato pizza and Grandma's Spudnuts *(Idaho donuts)* flitted through her mind. All was quiet except for someone walking down the hall talking on their cell phone.

Early in the morning, someone complained of a strange odor coming from Room 321. Security broke through the door to find the stiff body of Anne Marie overcome by fumes, her red braids lying on the pillow and potato chips smashed all over the bed.

****POLICE REPORT****

Sheriff Mark McCullum was called to investigate yet another death at the Cambridge Ritz-Southgate, with Coroner Jane Brickwall arriving close behind. This time, it appeared that there was a computer chip placed in a bag of potato chips under the bed of one Anne Marie Gableton, world famous chef from Prince Edward Island.

"This is the kind of explosive chip that is often set off by a cell phone," said McCullum. "The computer chip was in the bag of potato chips. This is the first time I ever heard of getting your life crushed by a potato 'chip.'"

McCullum told Dr. Brickwall that a suspicious person was seen walking the hall earlier, talking on a cell phone. Witnesses said they weren't sure if it was a man or woman, but the person wore an orange jumpsuit and used the name "Diddy."

"What's that?" McCullum asked as the coroner retrieved a crumpled wad of paper from the bedroom floor.

Unfolding the paper, she discovered handwritten notes. It read, "Question: Do you know what to do with a three-hundred pound potato? Answer: You just butter it up."

"Oh, man," groaned McCullum. "Are we dealing with a killer who likes to tell wacky jokes?"

"Apparently," said the coroner. "On the other side, the killer wrote, 'I'd never let my son marry Katie Couric, because she's just a common-tater.'"

Then Dr. Brickwall pointed to the mirror, where the killer had left a lipstick message saying, "Anne Marie didn't know potatoes. She was just a small fry."

"I hate food jokes," McCullum muttered, "but I can't resist—it looks like we have a cereal killer on our hands."

A Disloyal Royal

Slowly easing its way through Cambridge, the stretch Greyhound limo of Prince Arnold turned onto Southgate Parkway. Escorted by five cruisers from the Cambridge Police Department, they were joined by sheriff's deputies as they crossed Interstate 70.

"Driver, driver," shouted Prince Arnold, "Why are we going away from the resort? Are you lost?"

"No, Your Highness, the police are directing us to park at the airport. Our vehicle is too large for the parking lot at the Cambridge Ritz-Southgate. They are sending a smaller limo to pick us up."

Large hardly described Prince Arnold's limo, which was a Greyhound bus stretched to over one hundred feet in length. "Super Dog," as it was called in his country of Burkina Faso, was built like an armored tank and powered by two Mercedes Benz-600 ZHI engines. It had a top speed of one hundred twenty miles per hour. The interior, designed by the Prince himself, featured a full bath with solid gold fixtures, a four-star restaurant adjacent to a large recreation room equipped with a four hundred-inch flat screen TV, and a bowling alley.

Arnold was raised by missionaries after his parents were killed in a plane crash. Recognizing his talent for cooking, they arranged for him to study in Ethiopia and the internationally acclaimed Chad Culinary School in Chez, Chad. After graduation, he returned to Burkina Faso in Africa and became the personal chef of King Blusho.

Adopted by the king after the unexpected death of his only son, Arnold quickly adapted to royalty. Palace rumors were that Arnold administered small amounts of arsenic to the King's son to induce a fatal heart attack. Following the traditional burial rites for royalty in Burkina Faso, the body was cremated thirty minutes after his death, thus eliminating any chance of an autopsy or a police investigation.

Over the next few years, Prince Arnold, or "Arsenic Arnie" as he was now known around the palace, perfected his exotic recipes. His most famous was "Lizard Au Jus," lizard gizzards wrapped in palm leaves and served over a bed of rice in a garlic and lemon sauce.

When the Sheik invited Arnold to participate in the Cambridge International Cook-off, he was urged to do so by King Blusho.

"You can bring fame to our small African country," said the King.

"Your Highness, what would I serve? And the distance is great. You know my fear of flying."

"Take the limo, my son; it has all the comforts of the palace. Serve some of your famous cobra stew or, better yet, one of my favorites, sautéed monkey brains, served with unborn corn and beetle sprouts."

Once settled in his suite on the second floor of the Ritz-Southgate, the Prince checked his itinerary. *Ah*, he thought, *I have time to acquaint myself with local customs.*

Early the next morning, over a breakfast of grilled grasshoppers and robin eggs, the Prince was summoned to the door. "Your Highness, this man says he knows you. He is quite persistent," said the security guard.

Looking over the head of the guard, Prince Arnold saw an old friend. "Ron, Ron, come in! How long has it been? Let me see…ah, yes, it was three years ago in Rwanda. You were selling insurance to pirates. Sit and have some breakfast."

"No thanks, Your Highness. I'm afraid I'm here to ask a favor."

"What can I do for you?"

"I have come to invite you to be the guest speaker at our Big Cat Club lunch on Monday."

"Ah! The Big Cat Club. I am familiar with their work. Many of my countrymen have received free eyeglasses through your organization. I would be happy to attend."

"We meet downstairs in a small banquet room between the main dining hall and the kitchen," Ron said.

Following lunch with the Big Cat Club, the Prince was introduced by Big Cat President, Len Cahoot.

Grasping the podium, the Prince thanked Len for his kind words. "I know you want to know what dish I will prepare for the cook-off," he said. Pausing for a drink of water, he continued, "I'll be serving my newest creation, a lightly buttered…" Stopping in mid-sentence, he gasped. Grabbing his throat, he pointed at a group of waiters huddled in a corner before toppling across the table, spilling half-eaten food and dirty dishes to the floor.

"Is there a doctor in the house?" someone shouted.

"I'm not a doctor," shouted the tail turner, but I stayed at a Holiday Inn Express last night." Bending over the body, he looked up, shaking his head. "He's gone," he said. "He's gone."

**** POLICE REPORT****

Pushing his way through the crowd, Police Chief Ricky Tate was stunned to see Sheriff Mark McCullum standing over the body. "I believe this is in my jurisdiction, Mark. Please move back," he said.

"Easy, Ricky, I'm not trying to steal your thunder. I just dropped by for lunch, and this happened."

"What went on here, Mark? Did you see it?"

"Like I said, Ricky, I just stopped for lunch. I didn't know anything was wrong until I saw him fall."

Turning to face the crowd of shocked club members, Tate asked for quiet. "I'll need everyone who was sitting at the front tables to stick around. The rest of you, please go home. If we need you, we will call you."

Turning, Tate kneeled beside the body. McCullum squatted down on the other side. "You know, Mark, this doesn't look like an ordinary heart attack," the chief intoned.

"What can I do to help, Ricky? Pardon the pun, but we are getting buried in dead chefs."

"Well, for one thing, Mark, you can call the coroner, Dr. Jane Brickwall, and get her down here. We need to secure this area. Why don't you have the deputies eating donuts outside tape off the area? We don't need a bunch of sightseers and photographers taking pictures and embarrassing us again."

"I don't get it, Mark. You sure you didn't see anything unusual?"

"Nothing, Ricky. With the Prince being here, the building was packed. You might want to question the restaurant manager, Alf Wee. I don't know for sure, but, like I said, he was dead before he hit the floor. And look, rigor mortis is already setting in. He has only been dead twenty minutes. Smell his mouth and see if you think what I'm thinking."

Both bent over to smell the Prince's mouth. McCullum stood up, saying, "Arsenic, Ricky. It smells like arsenic."

"I know. I haven't smelled arsenic since I investigated the Jonestown suicides. But how did he ingest arsenic?"

"There must be ten cooks in the kitchen and another ten people who served the meal," McCullum said, his eyes narrowing. "Take your pick."

LUTFISK-LEFSE LEADS TO LUNACY

Sven Ingebretson and his entourage arrived at the Cambridge Ritz-Southgate luxury hotel for the Cambridge International Cook-off, lured by the millions in prizes offered to the winner. Sven was in dire financial trouble, the result of years of misconduct in the romance department, and he was determined to win. It seemed that he loved well but none too wisely. The consequent alimony for six ex-wives and child support for eight children left him desperately short of kronas.

Last evening, Sven visited the hotel lounge, where he passed the time visiting with local boys Buddy Babbit and Larry Moffet. As the evening wore on and the drinks came faster and faster, Sven proclaimed for any and all to hear that he was the world's greatest chef. He knew it, his family knew it, "and soon everyone will know it," he shouted. The great success he had enjoyed in Sweden had swollen his head to massive proportions, and now he was ready to take on all comers.

Sheik Muhammad Shah Abdul Hussein had offered ten million dollars in prizes to the chef who created the most delicious, simply prepared dinner. Nothing exotic, nothing complicated; just simple down-home cooking. Sven meant to take home the prizes.

He planned the menu carefully. It would feature lutfisk as the entrée. Lutfisk is that sometimes misunderstood Swedish fish dish so beloved by so many. It is usually prepared with codfish which has been soaked in lye for some time. No one seemed to remember how it came about, but it was believed to have happened when fires went out and cooking fish were allowed to fall into the ashes. Someone, probably a person who was hungry—make that desperately hungry—thought it looked rather good, so they soaked the lye out of it, dried it, and took it from there. Or so they say. It had been around for so long no one knew for certain. Most chefs knew it was rather tricky to get the flavor just right, but Sven had perfected the process.

Getting the lutfisk into the United States was another matter. Sven knew it would be rather challenging, but when officials got a whiff of the stuff, they quickly passed it through customs, as no one wanted to deal with it. There's something about cod, soaked in lye for ages, rinsed, dried, and packed for traveling, that's a bit off-putting.

The lutfisk was to be accompanied by seasonal vegetables and lefse, a Scandinavian flatbread made from mashed potatoes. Very versatile, lefse is a staple in every Swedish home and is useful under many guises. It is said that in Sweden shoes are often resoled and leaky boots are sometimes repaired with it. Holes in walls, cracks in windows, the leveling of a wobbling table…you name it and it'll be lefse to the rescue. You betcha! In fact, lefse has been compared to our very own duct tape for its versatility. Sven had spent Friday morning at the farmers' market being held on the Guernsey County Courthouse grounds. A weekly occurrence during the growing season, one could purchase the freshest produce of the season. Sven was able to find everything he needed, plus a few items he was unfamiliar with.

The finishing touch to Sven's simple but delicious meal would be krumkaki, a sweet, fragile confection, beautifully presented, stuffed with freshly made ice cream and topped with various fruits. He had yet to check with his prep chefs, but Sven was confident that they had carried out his instructions and within hours he would be Sweden's national treasure.

As Tilly, the maid, prepared to make her morning rounds, she couldn't help but think about the lack of neatness from a few of the visiting chefs. She guessed they were used to other people picking and cleaning up after them, but a few of them were such slobs. *You'd never think that they could be so untidy. Why, the way some strut around the hotel in their finery, it's hard to believe they'd leave their rooms looking like a pig sty. Like that guy from that little province in the Middle-East, Whatchacallit? The silk suit, the colorful turban, and the jewelry—wow! Some of those rocks, if they're real, must have cost a fortune. Boy, if people could only see his room, they wouldn't want to eat anything he cooked.*

But it was time to get to work. Tilly reluctantly entered the first room assignment of the morning. Things around the Cambridge Ritz-Southgate had been crazy for the past few days and she was in no hurry to start her rounds.

When she first heard about the Cambridge International Cook-off, she was excited, thinking, *The tips should be good and, better still, I might get a chance to meet some exciting new guys. Most of them foreign chefs talk funny, but it'd be a nice change from the Southeast Ohio twang I hear every day.*

But now someone was killing off the visiting chefs and Tilly was getting weary of the messes left for her to clean up. *No point in putting it off*, she told herself. *Delaying won't change anything so I might as well get on with it. Besides, maybe this one will be OK.* Opening the door, she was met with a disgusting odor. *Nope, it smells like trouble, big trouble. I believe it's going to be another one of those days.*

There, lying on the floor in his PJ's, was Sven Ingebretson, battered, bruised, and bloody. Something resembling bread was stuffed into every orifice of his head.

"Here we go again," mumbled Tilly to herself. "I'm going to have a rotten time cleaning up this mess." Hands on hips, she observed the late Mr. Ingebretson once again, then dialed 9-1-1.

"Hi, it's me, Tilly. I got another one for you!"

****POLICE REPORT****

Sheriff Mark McCullum and Police Chief Ricky Tate greeted Tilly as they entered Suite 622. "Hey, Tilly, whatcha got this time?" asked the sheriff.

"Don't know. But this one really stinks, literally," she answered.

Covering his nose, Chief Tate said, "You got that right." Scattered around the room were several very dead, very stiff fish. Visible on the victim's face and head were the outlines of fish. There was no doubt that the man had been beaten to death with a large fish, splattering a lot of blood in the process. McCullum knew that identifying that stuff in the victim's mouth, nose, and ears could be the key to solving this case. It would take the forensics boys quite some time to get to the bottom of this one.

"There's something very fishy here," the sheriff murmured when Coroner Jane Brickwall arrived.

She smiled, "Just got the call. I knew you wouldn't want to do this on your own hook." Glancing at the dead man's beaten face, she added, "He took a whale of a beating."

"We can run some quick tests, but those dead fish don't look like anything I ever saw come out of Seneca Lake," McCullum said.

Swiss Miss On List

Thousands of area residents, lining Brick Church Road leading to the Cambridge International Airport, screamed with excitement at the approach of the jumbo cargo plane. The gleaming white giant with a large red cross on the tail—a Lockheed D-55 Galaxy—touched down easily, eventually rumbling to a stop only a few feet from the end of the runway.

Harry Lostego, the airport manager, wet with sweat and shaking like a bowl of cherry Jell-O at a church picnic, muttered, "What's a Swiss plane that large doing here?"

The rear cargo door banged open, releasing three figures riding black World War II German motorcycles, popular with the Gestapo. They roared across the tarmac toward Cambridge at well over a hundred miles an hour. Each sidecar held two giant Saint Bernard dogs, all tightly buckled in and wearing crash helmets. In less than a minute, the three bikes could be heard roaring south on Interstate 77.

The new paint jobs on the vintage motorcycles covered the Nazi swastikas on the sidecars, and the engines had been rebuilt for speed. The three bikers got to Caldwell in eight minutes, made a U-turn across the median, then roared northward. They pulled into the Ritz-Southgate parking lot nine minutes later. When the bikers removed their goggles, bystanders saw that the lead rider was an attractive woman. Her two companions were square-headed Germans with closely cropped blond hair. The bugs on their teeth were barely noticeable. The brisk ride had released some of the built-up weariness from the long trip from Geneva.

Back at the airport, a large U-Haul truck pulled up to the cargo door, where workers dressed in leather knickers unloaded six large cardboard boxes marked “Fragile,” each about five feet square. Minutes later, the workers, whose dress resembled the goat herders in “Heidi,” offloaded the boxes at the Cambridge Ritz-Southgate. The concierge noticed the boxes were bulky but surprisingly light. He shrugged. After checking in a number of Cambridge International Cook-off competitors from all over the world, nothing surprised him.

The newest visitor to the resort was Jenifer Dzsennifer, a well-known gourmet chef. She had learned the art of Central European cooking while in rehabilitation at a Swiss Gender Transformation Center in Geneva. Muscular, blonde, with blue eyes, she resembled the East German male weightlifters of years gone by, including the hairy chest. She was known worldwide for her wild boar sausage seasoned with borscht and acorns and served with chopped parsnips, lumpy sour cream, and grilled liverwurst.

Jenifer had reserved an adjoining suite for her six Saint Bernard dogs, each carrying two-quart casks of top-shelf brandy. She had a weakness for large dogs, good brandy, hot vintage motorcycles, and Swiss-made clocks. Winning the cook-off was a personal goal; the prize money wasn’t important since she was already extremely rich. Her father had been an important Swiss banker in Zurich at the outset of World War II. In 1940, knowing Switzerland would always remain a neutral nation, he visited Adolph Hitler at his Berchtesgaden hideaway to work out a deal with Der Fuhrer and his Nazi staff. Otto Dzsennifer would receive every deutsche mark the Germans could steal as they plundered Europe, promising total anonymity and huge interest on the deposits. He also vowed never to do business with anyone from the Allied nations.

Soon thereafter, in New York, Otto met with dozens of rich Wall Street investors, who stood to make millions cashing in on various aspects of the United States war effort. He gave the Americans the same deal and promised not to accept a single deutsche mark from any Axis power.

Working both sides of the street, he was a billionaire when the war ended. Afterward, he moved to Argentina to live out his life in obscene luxury. Jenifer apparently inherited his cunning intuition and competitive energy.

Only her two bodyguards knew the meal she planned to serve the Sheik would be a rich pastry made with egg yolks, cheeses, heavy cream, chocolate, boar fat, and butter wrapped in a crispy chicken skin.

She was still a trifle stressed after the long flight from Geneva. The breakneck motorcycle ride with her bodyguards to Caldwell, that took just ten minutes, helped calm her down, as did three large mugs of brandy. She popped two large red capsules, a blue one, and three yellow ones into her mouth, then decided to check on her boxes in the next room.

That's where her bodyguards, Klaus and Helmut, found her the next morning after hearing ear-shattering noises from the room. "It sounds like cuckoo clocks," shouted Helmut, slamming his huge body against the locked door, sending a thousand pieces of mahogany flying in all directions. Inside, they found Jenifer's broken body, bleeding from dozens of ugly head wounds. Blood trickled down all four walls to the floor. The backdrop in the horrid death scene was a hundred cuckoo clocks on the walls, crazily belting out "cuckoo, cuckoo, cuckoo..."

When local policemen arrived moments later, their first job was to disconnect the crass cacophony of cuckoo clocks.

****POLICE REPORT****

Sheriff Mark McCullum and Police Chief Ricky Tate led a contingent of investigators to the death scene, where they were greeted by six friendly, but slobbering, Saint Bernard dogs. The north side of the murder scene was inside the city limits; the south side was in the county. “Shut off those blasted cuckoo clocks,” yelled McCullum. “That noise makes me dizzy.”

“Terrible!” answered Tate, as he began ripping the noisy clocks from the walls and smashing them on the floor.

“And that’s exactly what happened,” interjected Dr. Jane Brickwall, the county coroner, slowly surveying the scene. “Someone rigged those clocks to go off simultaneously, then adjusted them to ‘cuckoo’ nonstop. Definitely murder, gentlemen. Someone locked the victim inside this room. After several hours, the crass cuckoo cacophony got the best of her and she cracked mentally.”

The cops stared at the coroner in disbelief. Dr. Brickwall continued. “The bloody footprints on the carpet show that she circled the room many times, ramming her head against the walls, causing the fatal injuries.”

“Holy smokes!” muttered Tate. “That would drive anyone...”

“Cuckoo, yes. The strident noise from a hundred cuckoo clocks caused this woman to kill herself with her own continuous head-bashing. I’ve never seen such a well-designed, diabolical murder plan. What we’re up against here, gentlemen, is clearly one of the most fiendish, sadistic killers of all time,” Dr. Brickwall concluded.

Please Don't Cut the Cheese

The diminutive, chisel-featured man with tousled carrot-colored hair and a pencil-thin mustache strode majestically through the doors of the Cambridge Ritz-Southgate. Trailing dutifully behind were his companions and apprentices, Jacques and Gilles, both of whom stood several feet taller than their mentor.

"Attention!" Jacques proclaimed to the assemblage in the grand entrance. "Presenting Jean-Pierre Benoît Rousseau, world-famous chef of Avignon Grand Hotel!" The beaming crowd applauded enthusiastically, pressing forward to meet the extraordinary little chef arriving from Avignon, France. He was here to take part in Saudi Arabian Sheik Muhammad Shah Abdul Hussein el al Hassid Aka Abba Al Said Udaba Uka's "World's Most Delicious No-Frills Dinner" Cook-off at the Cambridge Ritz-Southgate.

Strutting around the grand salon like a bantam rooster courting today's hen, Jean-Pierre spoke with each person briefly, kissing the hands of all the ladies. "Enchanté," he repeated fluidly, gliding through the crowd as enigmatically as a fox through a chicken coop.

As he approached the hotel desk, he crowed noisily, "Garçon! I am ready to see zee keetchen!" His disheveled mass of red hair quivered like a cock's comb as he stretched to his maximum height of 3 feet 4 inches and added pointedly, "At once."

After a leisurely tour of the kitchen and dining facilities, Jean-Pierre retired to his top floor suite, leaving his assistants to see to the customary adaptations he required. The hotel staff was quick to respond to the needs of the renowned and much admired chef.

After swimming a few laps in the hot tub, Jean-Pierre, swaddled in a plush hotel towel, sipped a glass of Chateauneuf-du-Pape as he perused the latest issue of Le Monde. Refreshed and informed, he slipped into his favorite peacock blue silk shirt and a custom-tailored heron gray Tom James suit.

His stay would be a hectic one. Jean-Pierre was the honored guest that evening at the Cambridge Performing Arts Center's presentation of the Zola play, *Thérèse Raquin.* A wine-and-cheese soirée afterward, hosted by Sean Piccolocaucus, lured Cambridge's elite. Jean-Pierre was at his charming best with the ladies. One exquisitely tall, slender maiden immediately piqued his admiration. Like a banty on a June bug, he leapt onto the barstool beside her to whisper in her ear, "Tu es magnifique, ma chérie. Mai je vous rencontrer demain pour le déjeuner?" *("You look wonderful, my darling. May I meet you tomorrow for lunch?")* She blushed, but nodded discreetly.

At Georgetown Vineyards in the wee hours next morning, Jean-Pierre savored a delightful Chardonnay as he surveyed the lights of Cambridge from the ridge above the Ritz-Southgate. "Mon Dieu, Monsieur Piccolocaucus, ziss iss marvelous! I must have a case, and four bottles of zat special extra virgin olive oil. Zee Sheik must have ziss wine wiss za meal I am preparing for zee competition."

The next morning dawned on a severely hung-over but anticipatory Jean-Pierre. Showering, he hummed the French national anthem, *La Marsellaise.* Meticulously dressed in a chartreuse pullover, dark brown slacks, and a dark leather beret, he admired his reflection in the mirror while he phoned the kitchen. His assistants were already at work.

"Jacques, I have an engagement. I will return at four o'clock."

"Oui, Monsieur." Jacques rolled his eyes amusedly at Jilles.

“Anozzer woman?” grinned Gilles when Jacques rang off.

“Certainement,” smiled Jacques. “Come, zere is much to do.”

Jean-Pierre swaggered in later, wearing a magnanimous smile. Climbing the steps on a specially-made stool, he donned his apron. Aigo Boulido (garlic soup) soon simmered, egg yolks were whisked, and Quartre Quarts, a traditional French pound cake, was blended with his signature twist—escargot. Everything made from scratch.

With the potatoes baking, Jacques positioned a wheel of Munster cheese on the slicing block, chopping off a large hunk.

While Gilles blended raspberry glaze, Jean-Pierre prepared chicken a la diable. His orange topknot bounced effusively as he popped petite pieces of poultry into hot olive oil.

“Voilà! Jacques, Gilles, fresh aprons before you serve zee Sheik, s’il vous plaît.”

“Oui, Monsieur Rousseau,” nodded Gilles. They raced for the laundry as Jean-Pierre turned his attention to the simmering glaze, the crowning touch for his pièce de résistance.

Cold hands clamped an ethered handkerchief over Jean-Pierre’s mouth and nose, plunging him immediately into a sea of startled submission. He could vaguely feel cold fingers, one in each ear, lifting him like a bowling ball to the countertop. The last thing he saw was the waiting cheese guillotine. One soundless scream later, a tousled orange head rolled onto the floor as the raspberry glaze began to boil over.

****POLICE REPORT****

“I-Ick!” grimaced Dr. Jane Brickwall, the Guernsey County coroner, as she surveyed the murder scene. “Look at the mess this raspberry glaze made on the stovetop!”

“Do you think anyone would miss a slice of that pound cake?” whistled Police Chief Ricky Tate. “Dang that looks good!”

“Sorry. No tampering with the evidence, Chief. You know that.” Detective Handy DeStrange looked longingly at the elegant dessert himself, then turned his attention back to the pint-sized corpse. “Cause of death couldn’t be much clearer.”

“I wonder if we’re ever going to catch a break and crack these murder cases. As usual, our killer has flown the coop,” Chief Tate commented ruefully.

Dr. Brickwall rummaged absent-mindedly for a piece of Dubble Bubble in the pockets of her lab coat. “His poor little red head looks pretty lonely, rolled over there all by itself under the dessert cart. Last night after the play, the Sheik’s harem tripped all over each other to run their fingers through that magnificent mane.”

“Aha!” interjected Chief Tate, exultantly eyeballing a small scrap stuck in the rung of the little chef’s stool. “Check this out. Looks like part of an embroidered handkerchief. Is that half an “M” there—or is it a “W?” Unless I miss my guess, I bet…yep, it smells like ether. Guess that made it much easier for the killer to keep our little Casanova under control.”

Jane popped her gum and grinned. “He was a feisty one, all right. You should’ve seen him in action. For a little guy, he could really shake a tail feather.” Her eyes glazed over in momentary remembrance and her lips curved into a subtle smile.

Handy looked at her a little cock-eyed. “Why, Jane…do I detect a hint of admiration for our illustrious mini-chef?” he cackled. “Don’t wanna ruffle your feathers, my dear, but tell me, just where were you last night?”

The coroner almost choked on her gum. “Uh, we…uh, dang you, Handy! All we did was bowl a few games at King Pin. That’s not a crime, is it!?” Then her eyes twinkled. “But I will say things would have really livened up around here if he had come home to roost permanently in Cambridge.”

A Snake Steak is a Big Mistake

José signed the Cambridge Ritz-Southgate Hotel registry with a grandiose title, El Grande Senor José Delgado Ramirez Trujillo Sanchez. He had made up this phony name simply to impress the Arabian Sheik. His real name wasn't José Sanchez; he wasn't Spanish, or even Mexican, although he gave his hometown as Acapulco.

He was just another reservation Indian from the San Carlos Reservation. His real name was Gato Flojo; this meant Lazy Cat. José was aptly named because he was very lazy and he liked to sleep in the sun.

There were several raised eyebrows among the news reporters covering the cook-off entry booth when he registered his signature menu with the Cambridge International Cook-off committee. Rattlesnake à la King was an unusual dish for this part of the world. Despite the committee's misgivings, José was assigned a room on the same floor as many of the other chefs.

Lounging in a sunny corner of his room, José let his mind drift back to when he first became enamored with the idea of being a chef. While working as a swamper in the Buckaroo Bar and Grill in Tucson, he had watched The Food Channel on the television every day. Right there, on the spot, he decided to become a great chef.

On the TV shows, every chef wore a clean white apron, they never had to scrub their own pots and pans, and they always finished their meal up just as the show was over. He figured it was just a matter of getting his timing worked out. It didn't matter to José that he knew next to nothing about cooking. After all, this was America, the land of opportunity. Most of those TV chefs probably did not know any more about cooking than he did.

All of his formal training came a few months later, courtesy of the Maricopa County Sheriff's office. After a three-day drinking spree in Wittman, Arizona, Gato was caught barbequing a goat over an open fire on the outskirts of town. Nobody cared much about the goat, but having an open fire in the tinder dry desert was a serious offense. The judge gave him ninety days in the Maricopa County Impound.

This was a large fenced area out in the desert that was used to contain convicts. The Impound was fenced with twelve-foot-high chainlink fence, topped with three feet of razor wire. The two-acre impound was home to ninety-six non-paying guests of Maricopa County and sixteen guards. Cactus, rocks, and rattlesnakes abounded in the enclosure.

Prisoner housing consisted of 24x24-foot blue plastic tarps draped over a clothesline strung between two posts. This was mostly for shade since it seldom rained in the desert. The beds for prisoners were just a thin single blanket; prisoners soon learned to lie on one half and pull the other half over them.

When he was being processed in, José told the guards he was a cook and was told to report to the kitchen. The kitchen consisted of an open-sided 12x24-foot canvas tent to provide shade for the cooks. It was during this ninety-day sentence that he developed his recipe for Rattlesnake à la King.

José discovered the larger the snake, the better the flavor. Boneless snake medallions were marinated in aguardiente and mescal blossoms for two days. After removing the meat, the marinade was brought to a rolling boil. Three small red potatoes were then dropped in for each serving. He brought the mixture back to a full boil for twenty minutes then removed the potatoes from the broth. To the broth, he added three finely chopped jalapeno peppers, a cup of diced onion, a cup of diced parsnips, half a cup of Worcestershire, and another cup of aguardiente. After it was brought to a boil, he added a cup of finely chopped mesquite beans. He thickened it with a little flour, let it boil for one minute, then served it hot over the browned rattlesnake medallions. The dish was garnished with the rattlesnake rattles and slices of cholla cactus leaves.

After doing his stint as a guest of Maricopa County, José migrated northwest to Wickenburg, Arizona, where he landed a job as a short order cook in an all-night diner. The job only lasted one week before the customers began complaining about the food. A job in Prescott lasted two weeks and he moved on to Flagstaff.

José was burning burgers at a greasy spoon café just outside of Flagstaff when he saw the advertisement for the Cambridge Ritz-Southgate Cook-off. He decided it was his big chance at last and started hitching rides eastward. With any kind of luck, he could be there in a week.

José was lucky hitching rides and he got to Guernsey County in just four days. To his dismay, he had discovered Guernsey County was in the middle of a shortage of rattlesnakes. To compensate for this problem, he called his brother in Arizona and asked him to ship him some rattlesnakes by FedEx.

When José failed to come down for dinner that first evening, the desk clerk sent the bell captain to his room to make sure he was awake. The captain knocked on the door loudly several times, then unlocked the door. When he entered the room, he found José dead.

****POLICE REPORT****

A preliminary examination of the body by Coroner Jane Brickwall revealed two punctures on the victim's neck that very closely resembled a snake's bite. This tidbit of information brought concerned looks from both Sheriff Mark McCullum and Police Chief Ricky Tate. Neither man had ever investigated a death by snakebite case. If it actually was a snakebite that killed the victim, what happened to the snake?

The officers gingerly conducted a thorough search of the entire room, bathroom, closet, and dresser without finding any clues except an empty wooden box on the floor. The box had two hinges and a lockable hasp fixed to the lid. The United Parcel Service label on the top of the box showed it had been shipped to José Sanchez from San Carlos, Arizona. There were two very small labels, one on the bottom and one the back of the box, telling the world the box contained venomous reptiles.

Perplexed, McCullum said, "Chief, how are we going to tell the night manager there might be rattlesnakes loose in the Ritz-Southgate? He'll go into panic mode."

Tate replied, "Better we have one crazy Pakistani on our hands than five hundred panic-stricken hotel guests, all demanding we do something."

McCullum took a deep breath. "Let's call in a snake expert. Hopefully, someone who knows all about snakes can tell us where to look for them in a huge hotel. Maybe we can find them before anyone hears about it."

Tate replied, "I certainly hope so. I get the creepy-crawlies just thinking about a poisonous snake being loose around town. The voters aren't going to be happy about it either."

An Egyptian Conniption

Awan Massri admired the colorful flora as he gazed through the limousine window. His native Egypt, though resplendent with ancient man-made wonders, could not compare with southeastern Ohio for natural beauty. No spindly palm trees here; but emerald grasses, kaleidoscopic flowers, and forests of majestic trees that nearly reached the heavens flourished throughout the hilly terrain.

He readjusted his black beret, making certain to cover the upper half of his forehead. When not wearing his traditional chef's toque, he always topped his head with a beret to cover the high, rolling forehead that had been such an amusement with his schoolmates. The bulbous forehead, along with wooly-worm eyebrows and a slender neck, earned him the nickname "Awan Ankh" in his early school years.

Awan and his crew had checked in at the opulent Cambridge Ritz-Southgate earlier in the day and quickly appraised the competition. The line-up of great chefs was impressive. The trick would be to come up with very simple, but tasty, food. This would not be a "slam dunk," Awan mused, with his penchant for American slang. But he was certain that his "Pyramid Meatloaf" would dazzle the Sheik's taste buds as nothing else he had ever sampled.

Ironically, Awan had learned his now-famous cooking skills only twenty-five miles from his current location. The owner of the Nile Valley Spa, where Awan was chief chef, had sent him to culinary school at Zane State College in Ohio to expand his repertoire of entrées.

Awan delighted in concocting many world dishes, always infusing them with an Egyptian touch. He made a delicious potato soup with goat's milk and his meatloaf called for camel meat in place of ground beef. After a television appearance on Rachel Ray's show, Awan Massri became a household name in the cooking world. The Sheik's invitation to participate in the international cook-off was the high point of Awan's prolific career.

He used a secret ingredient in his meatloaf, one that had caused him trouble during customs check at JFK Airport. The camel meat presented no problem, but the impala flank caused an uproar. Awan argued to no avail with customs agents who angrily shouted the phrases, "endangered," "what-the-hell-were-you-thinking," and, "No way, José!" He could not understand the last comment at all, as he certainly did not appear to be Mexican or Spanish. He left JFK without the vital impala meat, wondering what to do.

"Eureka!" he shouted at 30,000 feet above Pittsburgh, causing his assistant to spill his drink. "Mohammed," he addressed the startled man seated next to him, "I have the solution. When I lived in Ohio during my days at Zane State, I often saw impala-like animals running about. They were perhaps a little larger than impalas, some with branched horns and some with no horns at all. When they ran—and they were very fast—their white tails would stand upright like flags. Salt Fork State Park, which is only a few miles from the Ritz-Southgate, is overrun with them. With my bow and saber, I can slay one of these animals and have the meat prepared in time for the cook-off."

Awan glanced at his wristwatch: two-thirty in the afternoon. Plenty of time. Mohammed steered the limo through the winding lanes of Salt Fork State Park.

"Here! Stop here!" Awan ordered when they came upon a heavily wooded area. He jumped out, bow in hand and saber dangling at his side.

"I'll call you as soon as I get one," Awan said, patting the cell phone in his pocket.

"Happy hunting!" Mohammed called as he watched Awan disappear into the woods.

After treading a mere 50 yards, he saw them: three deer under a crabapple tree, grazing contentedly. With careful stealth, he lowered to one knee and prepared the bow. As he began to draw back the arrow, a sudden rustling of leaves behind him frightened the deer, sending them flying up the hillside with their hooves barely touching the ground.

"My meat!" Awan shouted, his disappointment overshadowing the footsteps and rustling leaves behind him.

Suddenly something seized his neck, pressing his windpipe closed. Awan dropped the bow and waved his arms wildly. He and his attacker fell to the ground, but the death grip around his throat did not weaken. He managed to turn his head enough to see the face of a hairy, ape-like creature. Its partially open mouth revealed glistening fangs.

As Awan slipped toward unconsciousness, a quick glimpse of the creature's eyes evoked his last mortal thought: *I've seen those eyes before.*

****POLICE REPORT****

"Strangulation. Absolutely, strangulation," Coroner Jane Brickwall informed Sheriff Mark McCullum after examining the body in the woods. "There are no animal bites or scratches, and the imprints on his neck indicate adult human hands."

The sheriff wiped his forehead and sighed. "Since they announced that darned international cook-off at the Ritz-Southgate, this county has had more murders than we've had in the past two decades. I'll have to hire more detectives just to keep pace with this sudden crime wave."

He raised his hand to brush away a cobweb. "What the heck is this?" Grasping what appeared to be a clump of brown hair dangling from a sapling, he rubbed the hair between his thumb and forefinger.

"What is it?" asked Dr. Brickwall.

"It certainly isn't from man or beast," answered McCullum. "Looks like something from a cheap Halloween costume."

The sheriff's face brightened in what Deputy Watson would call an "ah-hah!" moment. "Last night old Delbert Winley called the station claiming that while night fishing he'd seen Bigfoot walking toward the Stone House trail. We told him to sleep it off, that anyone who drinks as much booze as he does is bound to see Bigfoot or little green men."

McCullum rubbed his chin, deep in thought. "Watson!" he called to his deputy. "Call every costume rental place within a 100-mile radius and ask if anyone has rented an ape suit lately. I'm determined to get to the bottom of this."

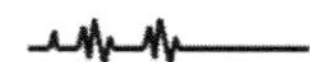

NASA Chef Hurled to Death

"'Это хорошо для работы правительства!' Do you know what that means? It's Russian for 'Good enough for government work!' And that's the *entire* report Vladimir e-mailed us this morning after realigning the nav platform's gyroscopes. That's no way to run a space station!" fumed Glenn Carpenter, NASA's Astronaut Office director.

He paused, reflecting. "You know, those endurance-testing Russians have been up there on the Space Station for six months now, and they've got at least five more to go. Keep this quiet, but we're going to give in to that idea they keep sending us for keeping them out of depression. We'll send up some Smirnoff on next week's shuttle. You design the recipes. Don't get 'em drunk—but go ahead and let 'em cook with vodka!"

Hearing those words, Chef Roy G. Biv's world changed dramatically. As NASA's chief designer of space cuisine, Chef Biv had been frustrated, up to that point, with the extraterrestrial limits imposed on his craft. There were only so many palatable things one could do with freeze-dried foods and Tang. But now...booze in space!? What a wonderful idea! And *vodka*, no less! The culinary options were endless!

Roy knew what he had to do. Within minutes of that meeting, his mind afire, he scheduled half a dozen cooking test trips on the Vomit Comet, NASA's weightlessness simulator plane.

The Vomit Comet, named in honor of an autonomic reflex that often occurs in zero-G, was a modified Boeing 727-100 jet aircraft used by NASA to produce true weightless conditions in half-minute bursts. Flying high parabolic arcs above the clouds, the plane would repeatedly dive toward the ground in perfect tandem with the tug of gravity, letting its occupants float free for 25 seconds at a time. At the bottom of the arc gravity returned, redoubled until the next dive, minutes later. It was the only place Chef Biv could taste test on the latest space stoves.

The Comet came to its present work with a most unusual history. Since pulling out of half-minute parabolic dives toward earth put great stress on a plane's fuselage, NASA quietly chose an aircraft stress-tested at speed in adverse flying conditions. Deep beneath the circular, blue, star-spangled NASA logo on the Vomit Comet's tail lay the long-ago registration code of Northwest Orient N467US. This was the legendary plane once hijacked by D.B. Cooper!

D.B. Cooper was the alias used by the only U.S. airplane hijacker ever to get away with the money and never be caught or even identified. Some forty years before, Cooper had boarded a commercial flight to Seattle then threatened to blow it up unless he received $200,000 and three parachutes. His demands met, he forced the crew to open the tail stairway in flight. Loot in hand, he'd vanished into a dark Oregon night, never to be heard from again. An airframe that could take that kind of punishment was exactly what NASA needed. Besides, it made a great cocktail party story!

Strangely named, Chef Roy G. Biv had long ago grown accustomed to quizzical looks when introduced to others. "Yes," he would say, "you heard right. I'm named for the rainbow mnemonic: red, orange, yellow, green, blue, indigo, violet. In fact, my dad wanted my last name to be 'Bivux' because ultraviolet and x-rays follow violet, though our eyes can't see them. But Mom put her foot down, saying 'Visible light only!' Mom and Dad were kind of strange."

Roy learned to cook by campfire at communes as his peripatetic parents drove their flower-powered minibus around the country seeking paths of enlightenment. Feeding strange people who travel a lot prepared Roy well for feeding astronauts.

The trick of space cooking, when not wimping out with a microwave, was to keep hot air flowing over the food without the use of a flame. When cooking with vodka for cosmonauts, the further trick was to apply heat long enough to lose the alcohol content through evaporation, while conversely intensifying the savory taste of a good, stiff drink in whatever food was under preparation. Scrambled eggs a la Smirnoff was a favorite.

The Russian cosmonauts were not just grateful for their vodka-laced meals, they were enthusiastically ecstatic. In no time flat, they began responding like Pavlov's dogs to the dinner bell. The first time Vladimir e-mailed Glenn Carpenter a message saying "Я сделаю еще один выход в открытый космос для водки-маринованная курица," *("I'll do another space walk for vodka-marinated chicken.")*, Glenn broke out laughing, framed the note, and put it on his wall.

NASA's decision to send Chef Biv to the Cambridge Ritz-Southgate International Cook-off was partly publicity stunt and partly a desperate attempt to make up for federal budget cuts, should he reel in the grand prize.

Following a brief delay to let a rain squall pass, the Vomit Comet took off from Cambridge International Airport at 9:18 a.m. on the last day of competition. Ascending rapidly to thirty thousand feet, the plane arced over and made its first plunge. As the Comet pulled out of its dive to head skyward again, horrified onlookers watched as the Boeing's aft stairway, tucked directly beneath its tail section, canted open. In the shock and whirl of cabin depressurization, Roy grasped in vain for a handhold. A lone figure was seen to tumble out and earthward from the plane, coming to its final rest just a few feet west of I-77 on the lawn of the Shenandoah crash site memorial, several miles south of Cambridge. Chef Roy G. Biv was dead!

****POLICE REPORT****

Sheriffs' offices in three adjoining counties; Guernsey, Noble, and Muskingum; coordinated efforts to solve an apparent murder. Sheriff Mark McCullum was first to receive a call at 9:30 a.m. reporting that room cleaners had found a man bound and gagged inside his closet at a local motel. The man, once freed, stated he worked as a pilot for NASA. He was knocked unconscious by an unknown assailant, who tied him up and stole his pilot's uniform.

An hour later, McCullum received a call from the Noble County sheriff, asking if he knew anything about a guy who fell out of the sky near the Guernsey-Noble county line, wearing a big, puffy, white hat. At 11:20 a.m., Don Breedem, director of animal management at The Wilds, called Muskingum County's sheriff to report, "Some nut landed and abandoned a 727 on our brand-new mile-long cheetah run. The cats are out there slashing its tires right now!" Muskingum, aware of the possible Cambridge fly-in connection, alerted Guernsey.

McCullum quickly put two and two and another two together, crafting a single, unifying crime scenario with the help of the bound pilot's report. "The hotel registration for Chef Rainbow Boy here says his middle name is 'Garland' and he's from Topeka. In 'Toto,' this means he ain't in Kansas anymore!" Grinning at his own wit and cleverness, McCullum broke into song:

"Somewhere over the rainbow, Fell this guy.
Crooks flew over the rainbow! That's why the chef here died!"

Revered Cafetero Feared Disappeared

Paddling down Leatherwood Creek in a canoe, the dark-skinned man with flaming red hair and green teeth whistled a happy tune. Always wearing a green Goiás football jersey, his head was topped off with a red magical hat.

Jose Carlos from Brazil felt he was arriving in style at the Cambridge Ritz-Southgate resort, as he was accustomed to paddling down the Amazon River every day. His red-capped parrot, Cherry, sat on his shoulder. As they traveled down Leatherwood Creek, Cherry squawked when he saw a group of boys wearing Bobcat t-shirts. "Why are coffee beans like teenagers?" Jose asked his parrot.

"Why? Why?" responded Cherry.

"Because they are always getting grounded," answered Jose, his green teeth flashing in a big smile.

In his bag, he carried the famous coffee beans from Brazil that would make him the top chef with his special Sweet Jose's Red-Capped Espresso. Brazil is the world's largest coffee producer and Jose was confident of victory. After all, he was the winner of the Gourmet Cup competition there for the last two years. Besides, he was a nephew of Juan Valdez and still took care of his uncle's donkeys even after Juan got too old to make TV commercials.

They grow an awful lot of coffee in Brazil, and this particular Bourbon Santos blend had a nutty, sweet, exceptional chocolate taste that everyone loved in his hometown of Pedregulho. Jose's zippered bag was filled with all the essentials to produce the best cup of coffee in the world. Inside were the special coffee beans picked from coffee trees where he worked, enclosed in a glass container to maintain freshness. Of course, he brought his own roaster and grinder, as nothing but the freshest ground beans produced the perfect cup of coffee.

The magical red hat that Jose wore would grant a wish to anyone who could take it from his head. Cherry often played a joke on his owner by flapping up from his shoulder, grabbing the red cap in his beak, and swooping off with it. As a result, Cherry always got her wish, a free ride on Jose's shoulder wherever he went.

"Do you know what kind of coffee was served on the Titanic?" Jose asked as he pulled the canoe onto the bank of Leatherwood Creek directly below Mr. Wee's Family Restaurant.

"What? What?" squawked the happy Cherry.

"Sanka," laughed Jose.

Headed up the creek bank to get a fresh cup of American coffee, Jose's feet made a strange impression. They were on backwards. His heels pointed forward; his toes pointed backward. If you were tracking him, you wouldn't end up where Jose was, but where he had been. The backward foot disease was traceable back hundreds of years to pygmies known as Florsheims. So Jose was pretty untraceable. You could tell he drank lots of coffee, as he moved faster than the Energizer bunny.

After three cups of coffee at Mr. Wee's, Jose hurried along to the Ritz-Southgate singing:

"Way down among Brazilians
Coffee beans grow by the billions,
So they've got to find those extra cups to fill.
They've got an awful lot of coffee in Brazil...
A politician's daughter was accused of drinking water
And was fined a great big fifty dollar bill

They've got an awful lot of coffee in Brazil...
You date a girl and find out later
She smells just like a percolator..."

As he hurried down the parkway on his backward feet, he thought about how he would use the cook-off prize money to purchase and manage the Goiás Football Club near his home in Brazil. He had dreamed of playing football, the most popular sport in Brazil, all his life but his feet made that impossible.

All the chefs were gathered in the banquet hall for a coffee break when Jose arrived at the Ritz-Southgate. One lady, a well-known chef from Switzerland, remarked, "This coffee is terrible. It tastes like dirt."

Jose quipped, "It should...it was ground this morning."

After reading the book, "O Saci," one competing chef learned the secret of Jose's red hat and quietly thought, *Today, I will get that red hat, and my wish will be to remain the best chef in the world.*

When Jose approached the table with the huge coffee urn, someone in an orange waitress uniform bumped into the urn, upsetting the hot contents directly on Jose. But then...there was no Jose to be found. It was as if he had melted away. Perhaps he did, or perhaps he just mysteriously vanished and was still roaming the hotel.

****POLICE REPORT****

The disappearance of Chef Jose Carlos was mystifying. He was there one minute and gone the next after an urn of hot coffee was knocked in his direction. Either he disappeared or melted away. The verdict was still out on that.

Coroner Jane Brickwall meticulously studied the scene, then said, "It seems either one could be a possibility. There is a legendary creature from Brazil that can disappear at any moment. Jose Carlos appears to fit the description of that character. We are continuing to investigate the possibility that he is still in the building. Since there is no body, my job is finished for now."

Just then, Cherry swooped by with something red in her beak. Could it be Jose's red hat? Would this mean that perhaps Jose had not melted away?

The perplexing disappearance caused a stir in the over-worked, sleep-deprived Guernsey County Sheriff's Department. How could murder be proven without a body? Sheriff Mark McCullum met with his staff at the scene to discuss the matter. It was known around the county that he was so tough that he ground coffee beans with his teeth.

One deputy, looking at the huge pool of spilled coffee on the floor, exclaimed, "That was a waste of good coffee. I could drink a cup or two right now if somebody would order some donuts from Kennedy's."

No one laughed.

"You know, when you're the sheriff, the best part of waking up is..."

"Now we're percolating," another deputy muttered.

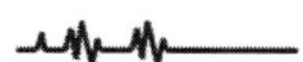

A Smidgen of Commie Makes Soup Just Like Mommy

As the plane banked sharply over the Cambridge International Airport, the bright red star on the tail of the MiG-25 glistened in the morning sun. Touching down moments later, the jet was escorted to the security zone of the Ohio National Guard by units from the Cambridge Fire Department.

After sliding down from the rear cockpit, Captain Youri Andropo walked to his waiting limousine. Surrounded by KGB agents and political officers, he was escorted to the Cambridge Ritz-Southgate.

Youri was born in Ukraine in the small Russian town of Yaki-Baneau. His father managed a large collective farm for the state. They lived in the only modern house in town, modern meaning they had a roof that didn't leak. Life was hard in this part of Russia. Youri saw the hard lines on his mother's face and the stooped shoulders of his father and vowed not to be the same.

School was easy for Youri. His excellent grades caught the attention of the local political commissar. Soon he was accepted into the Red Cadets, a steppingstone to the Supreme Soviet Aeronautical Academy. Upon graduation, Youri was commissioned a Captain in the Russian Air Force. When his squadron was transferred to a combat unit in Afghanistan, he became the proud commander of a Hind helicopter gunship.

During a fierce engagement, an RPG slammed into his ship, severely disfiguring him and ending his flying career. It was while he was recuperating in the hospital that he became addicted to TV cooking shows, especially "Emerald Live."

Following his discharge, Youri used his political connections to secure the exclusive rights to open his own restaurant chain, *Soups Are Us*. Starting with a basic cream of reindeer bisque and hot Ukrainian borscht, he graduated to his famous yak chowder—chunks of yak cooked in buttermilk and vinegar with potatoes and a dash of A.1. Steak Sauce. It wasn't long until he was known as the Soup Czar of the Soviet Union.

When invited to the cook-off at the Cambridge Ritz-Southgate, Youri saw an opportunity to market his soups in America. Although a devout communist, the recent collapse of the Soviet Union was rapidly converting him to the capitalist ways of the West.

Arriving at the main entrance to the Ritz, the crowd gasped at his disfigurement. "I know my body is wretched and pathetic," he said. "But make no mistake, my mind is sharp. I plan to win the heart of the Sheik with my soup recipes."

Wretched and pathetic hardly described Youri's appearance. His face resembled a black plastic mask, his left arm and hand had the appearance of old, dried out leather. His fingers moved like those of a robot.

Escorted to the VIP elevator, he was stunned when the doors opened. Scribbled on the walls were several slanderous slogans: "Killer of Kandahar," and "Butcher of Backau."

"Call the hotel manager at once," Youri screamed at the KGB agents.

Running down the hall, hotel manager Mitch Metheney stared in disbelief at the slogans.

"Get those Afghan cleaning kids down here immediately," he shouted at his chief of security. "I want to talk to them."

"You have Afghan people working here?" Youri asked with a startled look.

"Yes," replied Mitch, "they are children from the families who operate the Afghan Rug Company, just east of town. They earn extra money for college by cleaning rooms. I don't understand; normally they are quiet and shy. I guarantee you it won't happen again."

"I will hold you to that promise, Mr. Manager," Youri said sarcastically. "There can be no interruptions. The kitchen must be available to me so I can prepare the Sheik's obed *(lunch)*. No one is to enter once I begin my preparations."

Early the next morning while walking down the darkened hallway, Mitch smelled the aroma of soup cooking. He peered through a small window. The kitchen appeared to be deserted. His suspicion aroused, he entered the kitchen and turned on the overhead lights. Mitch froze at the sight before him. Hanging upside down from the ceiling was Youri Andropo. His head was immersed in a large pot of soup.

****POLICE REPORT****

The cars of Sheriff Mark McCullum and Police Chief Ricky Tate nearly collided as they turned into the Ritz-Southgate. Running toward the rear entrance to the kitchen, McCullum was stopped by Tate.

"Look, Mark, we have a serial killer on our hands. What do you think about sharing responsibility in this case? It will take both of us to solve what is going on here at the resort. I'll square it with the mayor."

"Sure, Ricky, we need to find out who is knocking off all the chefs."

Entering the kitchen, the pair stopped to observe the crime scene. With the exception of the body hanging from the ceiling, everything was neat and in order.

Pulling his cell phone from his pocket, McCullum asked Tate to secure the area with officers at the doors while he called Dr. Jane Brickwall, the county coroner.

"Tell them to keep a lookout for that Jeff photographer. We don't need him nosing around," he said.

Carefully studying the body, the duo was stunned by the scene. The deceased was bound with a multicolored cord, hanging by his feet from the ceiling. His head was immersed to the shoulders in a simmering pot of yak chowder.

"I've seen a lot of ways people get murdered, Mark, but this one takes the cake."

"You're right, Chief, but it sure is a waste of a good pot of yak chowder." Mark looked at the pot of soup on an adjacent stove. After he tasted a spoonful, he motioned for one of his deputies to come over.

"Take this pot of soup and that loaf of Russian black bread back to the office," McCullum said.

"You onto something, Mark?" Tate asked.

"No. I missed my breakfast this morning, and that cream of reindeer bisque sure tastes good. No sense letting it go to waste."

"Why do you think the head was left in the pot of hot soup?" Tate asked.

"I have a couple of ideas on that. One is to delay rigor mortis. The other is that the secret condiment in Youri's soup is a commie. You know, seasoned with eleven different herbs and commies...just joking, Ricky; I'm just joking," McCullum smiled.

"I know one thing that isn't a joke, Mark."

"What is that?"

"The cord that Youri is trussed up with is made out of the same material as the Afghan rug in the main lobby!" Tate said.

José, Can You See?

The Cambridge Ritz-Southgate hadn't yet opened when Tilly Taylor was hired to the housekeeping staff. From the beginning she worked hard, took her duties seriously, and hoped to one day head up the entire department.

Tilly loved her job. Nice people, good working conditions, and plenty of opportunities to meet interesting people. Why, just this past Tuesday evening, she'd popped into the Arena Lounge, Cambridge's most popular hot spot, and had the good fortune to almost meet Señor José Rodriquez, a visiting chef, from Madrid, in Cambridge for the International Cook-off.

He quickly had everyone's attention. José was decked out in a suit of lights, the traditional bullfighting costume, complete with shining cape, which he flourished expertly. The ladies present were dazzled by his performance. The men? Not so much.

Right from the start, Tilly was smitten. He had her from "halo," as he charmingly greeted everyone entering the room.

Tilly was healthy, unattached, cute as a Mickey Mouse wristwatch, and looking for love. So was José. He was a renowned chef in his native Spain. Creating delicious, mouth-watering meals was his craft. But being a young, handsome, red-blooded Latino, romance was his passion. He always had time for the ladies.

Tilly had never seen such a handsome man. He sure didn't look anything like the guys she had dated. He was very well built; more like a dancer than a world famous chef. Black hair fell lightly over one eye as he slowly took in everyone in the crowded room. The ladies were lovely, and he decided that he had little competition among the gentlemen.

Earlier, José had meticulously planned his entrée for the cook-off, Castilian Duck, or Creole Castellano; simple and delicious. Absolutely fit for a king, or in this case, a sheik. He had checked out the Cambridge City Pond on his arrival and found no shortage of ducks. He referred to his list: butter, check; olive oil, check; pine nut oil, check; walnuts, check; chilies, check; toasted breadcrumbs, check; duck stock, check; honey, check; avocado leaves, check; anise seed, check; salt and pepper, check; and, the very secret ingredient, kept under lock and key: a tried-and-true aphrodisiac, check.

Simple food, simply prepared. That was the criteria. José was confident that he had an excellent chance of walking off with the prizes. Satisfied that he was prepared for the cook-off, he turned his attention to the next important part of his trip—a bit of "cruisin'." And he knew just the place to go, having checked out The Arena during his excursion to the city park. It was ten o'clock. He knew the place would be packed with lovely ladies. As he dressed in the torero costume, he smiled as he thought of the possibilities the evening might bring. José was sure he would cut quite a swath as he made his entrance into the place.

That's when Tilly saw him. *Wow! The man of my dreams. Where has he been all my life? Oh, I've been waiting for him always. It is fate; I just know it is. He's here and I'm here. Now if I can only get him to notice me. I wonder if he speaks English. Never mind, it doesn't matter. We'll just speak the language of love.*

Soon José was in the middle of the floor, dancing a sensuous flamenco executed so perfectly that it would have rivaled his hero, José Greco, in his best years.

José's mother, Maria, always the romantic, had named her son for the great dancer. She never missed a chance to see him perform and had spent many pesos following him around Spain, adoring him from afar. She was so enamored with the man, she enrolled young José in flamenco classes, spending large sums of money on costumes throughout the years.

And then came the great disappointment of her life. She learned that the great dancer came not from Spain, but was born in Montorio nei Frentani, Italy. And, to add insult to injury, he was raised from age ten in Brooklyn, New York, U.S.A. Brokenhearted, Maria threw herself off a bridge. Fortunately, the waters were low and she only broke her legs. José, whose feet constantly hurt from all that stomping, stopped classes and only danced on special occasions.

This was a special occasion. With a click of the heels and a pass with the unfurled cape, the number ended. There was silence in the room, then sharp gasps followed by thunderous applause as the onlookers rushed onto the dance floor.

Before Tilly could catch her breath and make her way to the light of her life, he was swallowed up by the crowd of admirers and whisked away.

Disappointed but not dismayed, Tilly vowed she would visit every hot spot in town until she found him. With renewed energy, she took off on foot, going in and out of places calling his name and declaring her undying love. *When he sees me, he will recognize me as his great love, the one he has been searching for all his life. I just know it. He will know it is me, Tilly. If only he sees me.*

It was the wee hours of the morning. The clubs were all closed when Tilly finally gave up and went home. *I'm so tired and I must be at work early in the morning. I just can't think about this tonight. I'll think about it tomorrow.*

Sleepy-eyed, but rejuvenated by the thought that today she would surely find José, Tilly arrived at his room at the Ritz-Southgate. She was ready to pursue her quest when she was met by Sheriff Mark McCullum and Police Chief Ricky Tate. She could tell by the looks on their faces that there had been another victim. “Oh, no,” she said. “Not him.”

****POLICE REPORT****

Unaware of the previous night’s happenings, the officers told Tilly the name of the latest victim. Brokenhearted, she told them, “...but you don’t understand. I saw him last night. I’m sure we were meant to be together. If only I could have found him, maybe I could have saved him.”

Dismissing the distraught girl until later, the officers continued with their investigation. “I never saw anything like it,” said the sheriff. “What are those things sticking out of this poor guy’s back, anyway? And what’s that piece of red cloth lying beside him?”

“Well, I’ve never been to a bullfight, but I used to read a lot of Hemingway,” answered Tate. “I think you call those things banderillas. They stick them in the bull’s back and they wobble around while the torero does his tormenting. Makes the bull rather testy, I imagine. It doesn’t kill the bull, but I can see where it would a man. Guess we’ll just have to wait ’til Coroner Jane Brickwall determines what actually killed him. By the way, how about that tale of love and romance Tilly was telling? You think that’s a bunch of bull?”

Police Feel Growing Pressure

More than thirty chefs had been killed at the Cambridge Ritz-Southgate in just two weeks and local law enforcement personnel were feeling intense pressure. Not only were the mayor and county commissioners pressing for some answers; the governor was sending stinging twitters and e-mails. Complicating matters even more were the contingents of FBI, CIA, Interpol, and Scotland Yard agents who were camped out on the front lawn of the Guernsey County Justice Center.

On orders from the mayor, Southgate Parkway from the courthouse to the Whiteside car dealership was closed in the afternoons to allow the Sheik to hold camel races. The camels were sheltered in a large pink tent in the Justice Center parking lot. Who was to clean up after the camels became a city/state issue.

There were tough e-mails from the U.S. Secretary of State, who pointed out that the murders in Cambridge were triggering riots on the streets of many foreign capitals. "Unless these crimes are solved and the killer(s) brought to justice soon, these international incidents will reach epic proportions," the last e-mail said.

Sheriff Mark McCullum and Police Chief Ricky Tate issued a joint statement saying every law officer in the county would double their investigative efforts. The Ritz-Southgate murder files now filled fifty-six filing cabinets.

A late-night meeting at the Justice Center brought together some twenty of the top investigators on the case, plus Mike Meilson, local newspaper photographer. Meilson surprised everyone when he said, "We've investigated everyone except the Sheik. Why not check the Sheik's background? We know nothing about him."

It was worth a try. Within the hour, Tate's skilled computer hackers had a report. "Listen to this," the chief said, reading the printouts. "The Sheik's oil wells are running dry. To preserve his way of life, he has set up a ghost company and invested heavily in the major restaurants chains in America. He's a major stockholder in Tom Evans, The Outrack, Cracker Bucket, Benny's, The Olive Seed, and Creamy Krisp Donuts. Possibly, the Sheik's goal for the cook-off is to get the best chefs in the world under one roof, then kill them off. That would mean more customers in his own restaurants."

"Well, it's worth checking out," McCullum told the group, "but I have my doubts. Let's keep pressing." For the next twenty-two hours, McCullum watched tapes of "Murder, She Wrote," starring amateur detective Jessica Fletcher solving crimes in Cabot Cove, Maine. He was grasping at straws, he knew, but perhaps he'd get some ideas from the old TV show. He rechecked the Complaint Book, looking for anything that might lead him to a suspect. Then he noticed that, in the past week, reports had come in from several Byesville residents saying a large, black car was seen cruising the streets at about three o'clock in the morning. No one got a license number, but one caller said the car bore Louisiana license plates.

Across the hall, Tate also was burning the midnight oil. There were several pictures of Ben Matlock on the walls and a large poster asking, "What Would Matlock Do?" Tate double-checked the report of a Clover Farm Dairy truck being hijacked on Southgate Parkway the previous morning. According to investigating officers, an armed, masked gunman unloaded a hundred and twenty pounds of butter and put it into the trunk of a large black sedan. The dairy driver couldn't identify either the person who unloaded the butter or the driver. The culprits fled, leaving all the other products in the truck. They showed no interest in the dairy driver's money or credit cards.

Who'd want to steal so much butter? Tate pondered.

McCullum had just filled his coffee cup when Tate, also with a cup in hand, entered the kitchen at the Justice Center. "Any luck?"

Tate asked, rinsing his cup for what would be his eleventh cup of coffee of the day.

"Probably not," McCullum sighed wearily. "I'm putting out an APB for a large black car with Louisiana license plates. Something sort of suspicious about that."

Tate thought for a moment, then offered, "Funny thing. About midnight last night I saw a Louisiana car over on the south side. There was a rear bumper sticker on it saying '*Laissec Le Bon Rouleau de Temps.*'"

"French for 'Let the Good Times Roll,'" McCullum interpreted. They say that a lot in New Orleans."

"There was some foreign writing on a front bumper sticker too," Tate recalled. "It said '*Manger Plus de Crawdads.*'"

"My French isn't so good but I think that means 'Eat More Crawdads.'" McCullum mused.

Tate's eyes narrowed. "You know, we might be looking for a French chef who likes crawdads..."

"And we have a hijacked butter shipment," McCullum chimed in. "So let's check the Ritz-Southgate and see if they have a chef registered for the competition who cooks crawdads in butter."

They made a quick call to security at the Ritz-Southgate, where a guard confirmed that a large black car with Louisiana plates and bumper stickers was parked in the rear parking lot.

"We're on our way," Tate shouted as he and McCullum raced for the door. Both tossed an excited salute to the life-size poster of Clint Eastwood saying, "Go Ahead, Punk, Make My Day" on the wall.

McCullum put in a call for every available deputy to report to the Ritz-Southgate, along with the local SWAT team. Tate summoned a dozen of his best officers. Everyone was ordered to encircle the resort but to stay out of sight.

The desk clerk checked his records. The owner of the Louisiana car had signed in as Emerald Logassee from New Orleans. He was in

202, the only three-bedroom suite in the resort. Seconds later, Tate and McCullum, backed up by a contingent of thirty-four battle-ready officers, didn't bother to knock. They wanted the element of surprise, electing instead to open the door with one powerful blow of a battering ram.

Bursting inside, they were confronted by a short, silver-haired lady, a kindly grandmother type. She was smiling from ear to ear and waving a pound of Clover Farm butter in each hand. "Y'all come in, ya heah now?" she drawled. "We're fixin' to cook up somethin' goooood!"

"Good grief," sputtered Tate, "you're that woman on that TV cooking show."

"Y'all right about that. I'm Paula Dream an' I'm serving my famous Savannah Egg and Cream Surprise."

"She could make it taste better if she put some crawdads in it," said a disheveled Emerald, clad only in polka dot boxers and a Bayou Bengals t-shirt.

"Put your hands behind your backs. You're both under arrest for the murder of thirty chefs," McCullum ordered.

"Look, y'all, we never killed nobody. All Emerald and I did was do a few little robberies. Ain't that right, Emerald?"

"That's right. I was just the driver. We took orders from the big woman who did all that killing," Emerald sputtered. "That's her room there," he said, pointing to a bedroom door decorated tastefully with silk flowers, bamboo sticks, and artificial palm fronds.

McCullum and Tate burst into the bedroom only to find it empty. They gasped in awe at the walls, covered with reed baskets, perfectly hand-pieced quilts, intricate tapestries woven from hand-dyed homespun wool, and exquisitely framed hand-embroidered pastoral scenes. Every piece of furniture was adorned with homemade doilies and fresh flower arrangements, including the lavatory in the bathroom. Everything was meticulously clean.

Before the lawmen could react, another famous TV personality burst into the room, a tight smile on her thin lips. “Holy smoke,” gasped McCullum. “It’s Marda Steward!”

“You got that right, cowboy,” Marda almost sneered. “And what Emerald and Paula told you about the killings is correct. They did a little legwork, boosted a few items, but I’m taking credit for neutralizing those phony chefs. World’s best chefs, my sweet patootie! The three best chefs in the world are right here in this room and...”

“…none of us were invited to participate in the cook-off,” Paula and Emerald shouted passionately in unison.

McCullum and Tate looked at each other in shocked silence. Finally Tate muttered, “So you killed thirty people for revenge?”

“You betcha. And I’d do it again. No one ignores me and gets away with it,” Marda snarled.”I just wish I had capped that miserable Sheik while I was at it.”

“Vengeance is ours!” shouted Paula and Emerald, joining hands and raising them skyward while McCullum struggled to handcuff them.

“OK, you’ve been guests of the Cambridge Ritz-Southgate; now you’ll be guests of the Guernsey County taxpayers at our nice jail,” Tate smiled wickedly.

“How’s the food there?” Emerald asked.

“Pretty good.”

“Well, y’all, I can fix crawdads in butter anytime you want. And I kin toss in some cheese and grits,” Paula grinned. “We’re talkin’ low country yum-yum, y’all.”

“And I can make doilies for all the prisoners,” intoned Marda as the trio was led away. “And maybe embroider the prisoners’ initials on their towels.”

******THE END******

EPILOGUE

With the three killers safely behind bars, life slowly returned to normal in quiet little Cambridge, Ohio. The Sheik's Gulfstream unceremoniously left town. Several hours later, sketchy reports said the jet crashed into the Indian Ocean after the pilot discovered a small pig under his seat. Local motel rooms remained filled with crime writers from around the world, each seeking grisly facts that might lead to a Pulitzer Prize.

Sheriff Mark McCullum announced he would not run for re-election that fall because he signed a two-year acting contract on CSI Miami. Likewise, Chief Tate took an early retirement to appear as a regular on "Law and Order." And it came as no surprise when Coroner Jane Brickwall moved to Washington to be a nightly news analyst on the Fox News Network.

Members of the Rainy Day Writers are still together and working on their next bestseller. And every now and then, in the hallways of the Cambridge Ritz-Southgate, they say you can still catch a glimpse of a red-capped parrot or hear the tinkling of a "borrowed" set of car keys.

*****

The Writers

Samuel D. Besket

Sam Besket was born in Cambridge, Ohio, raised in Lore City, and hasn't strayed far from the nest. One of his first jobs as a boy was delivering the Cambridge *Daily Jeffersonian* and Zanesville *Times Recorder* newspapers.

After graduating from high school, he served four years in the U.S. Air Force during the Cuban Missile crisis and the Vietnam War. His Air Force travels took him to one of the coldest spots in the world, Goose Bay, Labrador.

Returning home, he started working for the Champion spark plug company in 1968 and retired 39 years later.

An avid reader, he is a member of the Cambridge Lion's Club and has a guest column in *The Daily Jeffersonian.* Sam is a member of Cambridge Writers Workshop and its new affiliate, the Rainy Day Writers. He lists his favorite book as *The Longest Raid of the Civil War* by Lester V. Horwitz.

Sam and his wife, Carolyn, have traveled the United States from coast to coast, enjoy boating on Seneca Lake, and now do all the things they couldn't when they were working.

Rick Booth

Originally from Cambridge, Rick Booth recently returned to Guernsey County after 34 years of software engineering in New York and Philadelphia. A chemistry graduate of Princeton University, he was two years into preclinical training at Columbia University's medical school when a chance 1979 encounter with the then-new TRS-80 personal computer, loaded with a whole 100-millionth the memory in today's PCs, changed his career path.

Self-taught in computing, Rick authored his first book on high-performance computing in 1997. Intel Corporation subsequently recruited Rick to co-author a second book on their most complex processor to date in 2001. He spent most of the 1980s working at the Children's Television Workshop (Sesame Street) on newfangled educational computer games and applications, including early computer video systems. At a later video game company, he is best known for co-authoring the NES classic, *A Boy and His Blob*.

Rick credits his father, Russell, a well-known area author of history books and articles, with inspiring his own writing bug. They have recently begun trading off authoring monthly history articles for the local *Now & Then* magazine, which has been running the senior Booth's writings since the 1990s.

Rick is "way glad," since 2007, to be back on home turf now. His interests include etymology, computer animation, satellite spotting, Amtrak politics, and, of course, writing.

JOY L. WILBERT ERSKINE

Born to a military family stationed at March Air Force Base in Riverside, California, Joy L. Wilbert Erskine was a lucky passenger each time her father relocated to new duty stations in cities and countries all over the world. She later married a military man and her travels continued. For much of her life, she has been a gypsy of sorts, wandering from place to place with no permanent spot to call home. This wandering always led to opportunities to meet fascinating new people and explore interesting new cultures. In the process, she has lived a happy life and come to realize that home is a simple matter of the heart.

With this background and a natural aptitude for the language arts, Joy, now retired in Cambridge, Ohio, pursues the writing interests she has entertained since childhood. She is a guest columnist for *The Daily Jeffersonian* newspaper and belongs to the Cambridge Writers Workshop and its Rainy Day Writers affiliate. Her favorite authors are Gerald N. Lund, Stephen E. Robinson, and David Wroblewski. Joy's short stories have appeared in the anthologies, *The Day We Learned to Write and Other Acts of Madness*, *The Wills Creek Chronicles*, *The Wills Creek Trilogies*, and *A Wills Creek Christmas*. She is also writing her first book, a fantasy about a place called Menterdown.

Beverly Justice

Prize-winning author Beverly Justice, a Cambridge, Ohio native, graduated from Kent State University with a B.A. degree in English. She also attended the former Muskingum Area Technical College, currently known as Zane State.

Her poetry and short stories have been published in *The Daily Jeffersonian* newspaper and in national publications, including *Cat Fancy* magazine. Her favorite contemporary authors are Dean Koontz, Stephen King, and Mitch Albom. She cites Henry David Thoreau as one of the greatest influences in her life and has visited Walden Pond in Massachusetts, where Thoreau did much of his writing.

Beverly is a member of the Southeastern Ohio Civil War Roundtable and the Daughters of Union Veterans. She is active in animal welfare organizations and has six cats that provide her with endless inspiration. "God put cats into our lives to remind us that we are not the superior species," Beverly said. It is her love of animals that may inspire her to write a book on the subject.

She credits the Rainy Day Writers group, and especially Jerry Wolfrom, with promoting her development as a writer by offering encouragement during times of doubt and by showing through their own examples how writing can enrich one's soul.

Beverly is an avid physical fitness enthusiast and can be found at the Cambridge Fitness Center nearly every day.

Beverly Wencek Kerr

A native of Indian Camp near Cambridge, Beverly Wencek Kerr grew up on a chicken farm with the example of parents who worked hard from dawn to dusk. She attended Hopewell, a one room school. An only child, she was encouraged to enjoy life. Reading was one of her favorite pleasures, earning her the label "bookworm" and fledging a lifelong passion for writing stories and plays. At Cambridge High School, she won the American Legion essay contest and served as Jeffersonian JG editor. Her writing expanded to short essays at Muskingum College, where she received her degree in education.

Beverly spent many gratifying years as an elementary teacher in the Cambridge and Guernsey County School districts. After raising her family on the farm, she returned to writing in the form of e-zine articles, opening up a new world of opportunities. This passion for writing has been enhanced the last few years through Cambridge Writers Workshop, where her short stories were published in *The Wills Creek Trilogies* and *A Wills Creek Christmas*.

She still enjoys reading and often writes about her travel adventures in the U.S. and beyond. Read more of her stories at her website: www.gypsyroadtrip.com. She is currently writing articles and a novel about her family's experiences with Alzheimer's.

Most of all, Beverly enjoys spreading a little happiness in the world by helping others whenever she can.

Dick Metheney

Dick Metheney, born in Wadsworth, Ohio, has lived most of his life in Medina County. An avid reader and book collector, he has been known to read the labels on canned goods if there is nothing else available.

He has worked in an auto factory, trained as an apprentice precision grinder, owned a landscaping business, built and operated a horse training facility, raised cattle, farmed, drove a school bus, prepared income taxes, and worked in a steel mill for thirty-three years.

After retiring, Dick and his wife, Alice, moved to a small farm near Quaker City, Ohio, in Guernsey County. They have five children, seven grandchildren, and one great-grandchild. He farms full time and writes every morning but makes time for hunting trips to Montana.

Dick's first fiction novel, "If It Is God's Will," was published in March 2010. His second novel, "Santana's Revenge" was released in April 2011. Dick is a member of the Cambridge Writers Workshop and Rainy Day Writers group. He has numerous short stories published in CWW short story compilations.

DONNA J. LAKE SHAFER

Most of her life, Donna J. Lake Shafer has had a love affair with words, both written and spoken. Beside her favorite easy chair are dictionaries, including French, Spanish, German, and Italian-English plus Roget's Thesaurus. She remembers her father often stating, "If you don't see it, hear it, or read it, you don't know it. The person who doesn't read is no better off than the person who can't read."

A life-long "people watcher," she has traveled extensively in the United States, Canada, and Europe. She often calls on her travel experiences and the people she has met to create short stories.

After graduating Cambridge High School, she obtained a position at the then newly-opened radio station WILE, where she worked for several years off and on as an advertising copy writer. It was in that job that she learned that writing can entail considerable creativity and hard work.

Between the times of employment at WILE, she married, had children, and even switched careers when she entered the medical field as a lab and x-ray technician.

More recently, Donna has tried her hand at short story writing and is finding it to be challenging, sometimes frustrating, but extremely satisfying.

Over the years she has worked to instill a love of the written word into her children, grandchildren, and great-grandchildren. So far, she reports, it's working well.

Jerry Wolfrom

After fifty years as a journalist, Wolfrom, coordinator of the Rainy Day Writers, has a room full of certificates, plaques, scrapbooks, and memorabilia. He has worked on many newspapers around the nation, including dailies in Findlay, Columbus and Cambridge, along with high-circulation papers in Fort Myers, Cape Coral, and Fort Pierce, Florida. He has covered murder trials, space shots, wildlife in Central American rain forests, the Kentucky Derby, the Indianapolis 500, volcanoes, deep sea fishing in Costa Rica, and thousands of community events.

In 1988, he was inducted into the Journalism Hall of Fame at Bowling Green State University, his alma mater. As a student there, he was named top Ohio college columnist, and received the Golden Scissors Award as outstanding graduating senior.

A prolific outdoor writer, Wolfrom contributed regularly to three national fishing magazines. But his main interest has been humor. In that genre, he has written nearly five thousand humor columns, which have appeared regularly in both large and small newspapers in seven states. He retired as acting publisher of the Daily Jeffersonian, where he also served on the board of directors.

Among hundreds of his celebrity interviews are Kurt Vonnegut Jr., Jackie Gleason, Al Capp, Robert Dole, Gerald Ford, Bill Blass, Pete Rose, Woody Hayes, Beverly Sills, Suzanne Pleschette, John Glenn Jr., Paul Lynde, and Charlie Daniels.

RECIPES

TO DIE FOR

Gypsy Bev's Recipe for Life

Stir in laughter, love and kindness
From the heart it has to come.
Mix with genuine forgiveness
And give your neighbor some.

Chop one grudge in tiny pieces
Add several cups of love.
Dredge with a large sized smile
And mix the ingredients above.

Dissolve the hate within you
By doing a very good deed.
Dash in some help for any friend
If they should be in need.

The amount of people you can serve
From the recipe above
Is in the quality of its ingredients
And unlimited amounts of love.

~~Author Unknown~~

Appetizers, Beverages, & Breads

Due Process Dried Beef Appetizers

1 jar dried beef
Spreadable cream cheese

Spread cheese to edges of a slice of dried beef. Roll up and slice into bite size pieces. Spear with toothpick for sealing and for easy handling. *(Herbs may be mixed with cream cheese for different flavors.)*

Donna Lake Shafer
Rainy Day Writer

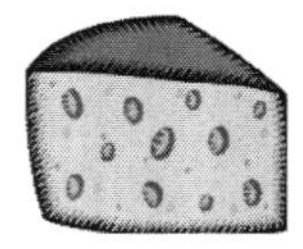

Clueless Cheese Spread

½ c. mayonnaise
½ c. sour cream
½ t. salt *(hickory salt preferred)*
1 clove minced garlic OR 1 t. garlic powder
1 T. chives
6 oz. shredded sharp cheddar
4 oz. shredded Swiss cheese
¼ c. beer

Blend. Refrigerate. Great on party rye or beer bread. Note: For smoother consistency, mix in blender.

Donna Lake Shafer
Rainy Day Writer

Alibi Artichoke Dip

1 can artichoke hearts, drained and mashed well
1 c. mayonnaise
1 c. parmesan cheese
Garlic salt to taste

Mix and heat slowly (325-350° F.), otherwise it will separate and be very oily. Note: Great Frito dip.

Donna Lake Shafer
Rainy Day Writer

Southgate Slush

46 oz. can pineapple juice
12 oz. frozen orange juice concentrate
12 oz. frozen lemonade concentrate
3 bananas (mashed)
2 c. sugar
4 c. water (divided)
2 qt. 7-Up
2 qt. lemon-lime soda

Mash bananas in blender with some pineapple juice. Dissolve sugar in 2 c. boiling water. Add remaining water and mix with frozen juice, bananas, and pineapple juice. Mix well and freeze. Take from freezer 2-3 hours before serving. Stir until slushy. Add 7-Up and lemon-lime soda.

Colleen Wheatley
Guernsey County Recorder

BAIL BOND BEER BREAD

3 c. self rising flour
2 T. sugar *(or honey)*
1 can beer at room temperature

Mix together and put into a greased loaf pan. Bake at 350 ° F. for one hour.

DONNA LAKE SHAFER
RAINY DAY WRITER

CRIME SPREE CRABBIES

6 English muffins, split and lightly toasted (set aside)
7 oz. can (approx.) white or claw crab meat
1 jar Old English cheese
2 T. mayonnaise
1 t. garlic salt
½ c. butter, softened
Dash of Tabasco sauce OR cayenne pepper

Mix all ingredients in a medium bowl. Evenly spread mixture onto muffin halves. Score each muffin half into fourths (do not cut through). Place on cookie sheet and put in freezer. When frozen, break into fourths and store in freezer bag until ready to use. (Hint: Always keep some in the freezer for emergencies.)

To finish: Place desired amount of frozen pieces on cookie sheet and bake 10 minutes in 425° F. oven. *DELICIOUS!*

DONNA LAKE SHAFER
RAINY DAY WRITER

THE "GRANDPA" SANDWICH

Peanut butter
Miracle Whip salad dressing
2 slices of bread

Everyone has heard of peanut butter and jelly sandwiches, but many are unaware that Miracle Whip salad dressing works well in place of jelly. A true mayonnaise can also be substituted.

The sandwich came to be known as a "Grandpa" sandwich in my home because it was the favorite sandwich of my son's grandfather, Russell Booth, since his own childhood in the 1930s. To distinguish it from more conventional peanut butter and jelly sandwiches, we had to coin another name. Though the ingredient list is simple, there are many variations possible, based on bread selection and thickness of application of the other ingredients.

Personally, I prefer the decadence of soft, white Wonder Bread with creamy peanut butter and a heavy dose of original recipe Miracle Whip. Others, in a Spartan mood, may opt for whole grains, chunky peanut butter, and light application of a variant like Miracle Whip Lite. Experiment and enjoy!

RICK BOOTH
RAINY DAY WRITER

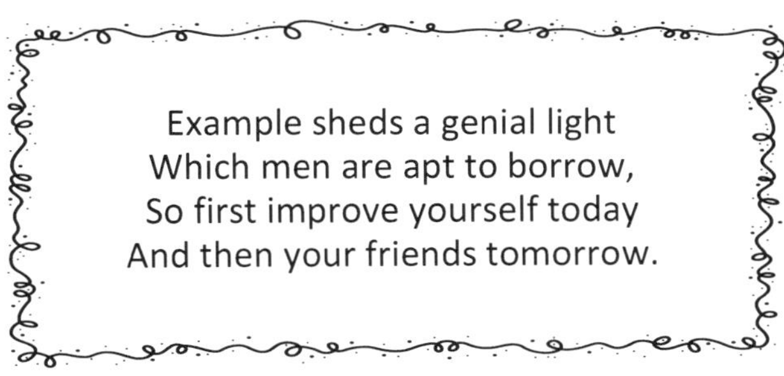

Salads and Vegetables

Southern Delight Festive Felony Salad

(No proper Southern meal is complete without a salad!)

½ c. sugar *(Sugar substitutes won't do for this Southern Belle!)*
⅓ c. cider or red wine vinegar *(for a little spice)*
2 T. lemon juice
2 T. finely chopped onion
½ t. salt
⅔ c. vegetable oil
2-3 t. poppy seeds
10 c. torn romaine lettuce
1 c. (4 oz.) shredded Swiss cheese
1 med. Granny Smith apple, cored and cubed
1 medium red pear, cored and cubed
¼ c. dried cranberries
½-1 c. chopped cashews

In a blender, combine sugar, vinegar, lemon juice, onion, and salt. Cover and process until blended. With blender, add oil. Add poppy seeds and blend. In a salad bowl, combine Romaine lettuce, Swiss cheese, apple, pear, and cranberries. Drizzle with desired amount of dressing. Add cashews. Toss to coat. Serve immediately.

ENJOY, YA'LL!

Debbie Robinson
Executive Director
Cambridge/Guernsey County Visitors & Convention Bureau

"To Die For" Six Cup Salad

- 1 c. pineapple chunks
- 1 c. coconut OR grapes
- 1 c. mandarin oranges
- 1 c. raisins
- 1 c. miniature marshmallows
- 1 c. sour cream

Mix all ingredients and refrigerate several hours before serving.

Pamela Harmon
Lifestyle/Obituary Editor
The Daily & Sunday Jeffersonian

Greek Salad

(by way of Athens, Ohio)

- 2 cucumbers, peeled and sliced
- 1 large tomato, sliced
- ¼ green pepper, sliced
- ½ jar of pitted Kalamata olives
- 4 or 5 leaves of romaine lettuce, chopped or broken
- 3 oz. feta cheese, crumbled
- Newman's Own light balsamic dressing

Mix together. Add dressing to taste.

Leslie Kleen, Columbus
(a.k.a. Les Kleen)
Ohio University music professor/composer, Retired

Kalisa's Jamaican Fruit Salad

(A tasty offering from "Honey Plan Stings Jamaican," by "Gypsy Bev")

3 T. Jamaican rum
2 T. sugar
2 c. kiwi, peeled and sliced
2 c. strawberries, sliced

In a small bowl, stir together rum and sugar until dissolved. In a large bowl, toss together kiwi and strawberries. Pour dressing over the fruit and toss to combine. Let stand at least 15 minutes before serving.

Beverly Wencek Kerr
Rainy Day Writers

Romaine Lettuce Litigation Salad

2 heads romaine lettuce, chopped
1 small can French fried onions
1 can chow mein noodles
Real bacon bits

Dressing:
1 c. real mayonnaise
2 T. white vinegar
½ c. sugar
1 t. celery seed

Prepare dressing and mix vigorously; add to lettuce. Add bacon bits (as much as you want); mix again. Add onions and chow mein noodles just before serving and mix once again. Easy and delicious.

Margo Johnston
Byesville Village Council

Capital Offense Carrot Casserole

1½ lb. carrots, sliced (4½ c.)
½ c. mayonnaise or salad dressing
2 T. chopped onion
2 T. prepared horseradish
¼ t. salt
Dash of pepper
¼ c. crushed saltine crackers (7 crackers)
2 t. melted margarine or butter

Cook sliced carrots in boiling, salted water until tender-crisp. Mix mayonnaise, onion, horseradish, salt, and pepper in a small bowl. Spread over top of carrots that have been placed in a shallow casserole. Add crushed saltines to the melted butter; sprinkle on top. Bake uncovered at 350° F. for 30 minutes.

Samuel D. Besket
Rainy Day Writer

Mum's Irish Champ

(From Chef Patrick McKenna in "Irish Host Becomes Toast")

2 lbs. potatoes, peeled, halved
1 c. milk *(or beer, if you're brave)*
1 c. green onions, diced or thinly sliced
½ t. salt
¼ c. butter *(try to use real butter)*
1 pinch freshly ground black pepper to taste

Place potatoes in large pot; fill with water to cover. Bring to a boil; cook until tender, about 20 minutes. Drain well. Return to very low heat; allow potatoes to dry for a few minutes. Heat milk and green onions gently in saucepan until warm. Mash potatoes, salt, and butter together until smooth. Stir in milk and green onion until mixed. Season with pepper. Serve piping hot, setting out extra butter.

Beverly Justice
Rainy Day Writer

Contempt of Court Corn Pudding

1 can creamed sweet corn
2 cans whole kernel sweet corn, drained
1 can sweetened condensed milk
2 eggs
1½ c. self-rising cornmeal mix
¼ c. molasses
¼ t. sea salt
¼ t. white pepper

Mix ingredients thoroughly and pour into bowl that has been sprayed with a non-stick spray (Pam, etc.). Bake in 350° F. oven 1 hour or until toothpick comes out of the pudding clean. *Note: Sometimes the baking dish can be set into a larger baking dish containing water. This will prevent the bottom and sides of the pudding from getting too brown before the center gets done. If this is done, add 1 hour to baking time.*

Dick Metheney
Rainy Day Writer

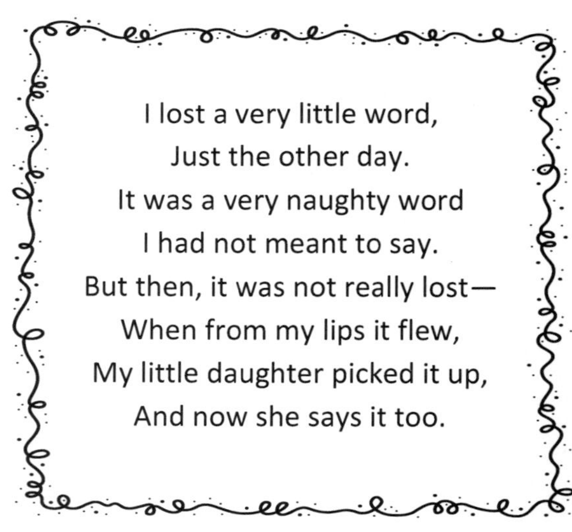

Soups

Serial Killer Cream of Crab Soup

1 lb. crabmeat
½ c. butter
¾ c. flour
2 10-oz. cans chicken broth
2 10-oz. cans cream of shrimp soup
2 t. Old Bay seafood seasoning
1 t. sea salt
¼ t. pepper
1 qt. fat-free half-and-half
¼ c. sherry

Melt butter in Dutch oven over low heat. Add flour, stirring until smooth. Cook 1 minute, stirring constantly, until thickened and bubbly. Add broth, shrimp soup, Old Bay, salt and pepper, and half-and-half. Cook 10-15 minutes on low heat. DO NOT BOIL. Stir frequently. Add crab. Add sherry right before serving. Makes 2 quarts. Serves about 5.

Daniel G. Padden
Guernsey County Prosecuting Attorney

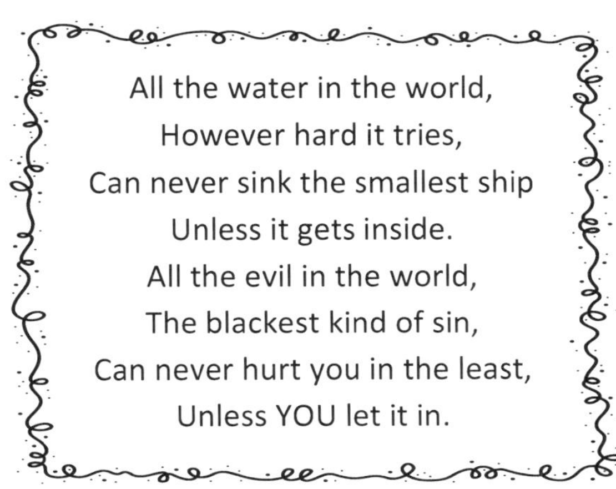

TIME-SERVED TACO SOUP

16 oz. can chili beans
16 oz. can kidney beans
16 oz. can black beans
8 oz. can tomato sauce
15 oz. diced stewed tomatoes
16 oz. can whole corn
16 oz. can creamed corn
1 pkg. taco seasoning
1 T. chili powder
1 lb. ground beef
1 onion, chopped
4 oz. chopped green chilies

Do not drain any of the canned foods. Add all ingredients to a crock pot except ground beef and onion. Brown ground beef and onion in a skillet. Add to crock pot. Simmer for at least 2 hours. Serve warm. Garnish with optional toppings: shredded cheese, sour cream, tortilla chips, or eat with large Fritos chips.

TONY BROWN
GUERNSEY COUNTY AUDITOR

LEATHERWOOD CREEK TURTLE SOUP

1 (10 or 12 lb.) turtle
1 head cabbage
12 cans Veg-All
1 gal. tomato juice
1 lg. onion, chopped
4 cloves garlic, crushed
½ lb. butter

Cook turtle meat 30 minutes; let cool; pick off bone. In water and tomato juice to cover, boil cabbage, onion, and garlic till done. Add turtle; let cook for about 30 minutes. Add butter last half hour also.

SAMUEL D. BESKET
RAINY DAY WRITER

Oyster vs. Artichoke Arbitration Soup

2 pts. oysters w/liquid/liquor
3 pts. chicken stock
1 can artichoke hearts, qtr'd.
¼ t. thyme
¼ t. white pepper
1 t. fresh chopped garlic
1 c. half-and-half
1 c. diced green onions
8 T. butter
8 T. flour

Melt butter in pan and add flour. Cook over medium heat for 5 minutes to make a white roux. Let cool and add chicken stock. Place over heat and stir until the mixture reaches a simmer. Add chopped garlic, thyme, and quartered artichoke hearts. Bring to a boil and add oysters and green onions. Salt and pepper to taste. Simmer for 5 minutes. Finish by adding 1 cup half-and-half. Stir. Enjoy! Serves 8.

Dan Beetem
(a.k.a. Don Breedem)
Director of Animal Management, The Wilds

Fireman's First Degree Murder Stew

1½-2 lbs. stewing beef cubes
Salt and pepper to taste
1 pkg. Lipton onion soup mix
1 can tomato soup
1 can cream of mushroom soup
1 can cream of celery soup
1 soup can of water
3-4 carrots, chunked
4-5 potatoes, chunked
1 can or 16 oz. pkg. frozen peas

Layer into at least a 5-quart baking dish.
Bake at 300° F. for 4-5 hours.
Do not stir.

Samuel D. Besket
Rainy Day Writer

Kelly's Irish Indictment Potato Soup

2 T. butter
4-5 medium green onions, sliced thin (about ½ cup)
1 stalk celery, sliced (½ c.)
1¾ cups chicken broth
⅛ t. ground black pepper
3 medium potatoes, sliced ¼-inch thick (abt. 3 c.)
1 c. milk
¾ c. cream cheese, softened

Heat butter in a 3-quart saucepan over medium heat. Add onions and celery and cook until tender. Add broth, pepper, and potatoes; heat to a boil. Reduce heat to low. Cover and cook for 15 minutes or until potatoes are tender. Add milk and cream cheese. Stir on low heat until well blended.

Jerry Wolfrom
Rainy Day Writer

Sentence Creole Shrimp & Crab Bisque

1 lb. can of real crab meat
4 T. butter
1 sm. onion, finely chopped
2 stalks celery, finely chopped
2 cloves minced garlic
⅓ c. flour
3 c. chicken broth
½ lb. steamed medium-size fresh shrimp, peeled, deveined, and chopped
1 c. cream AND 1 c. milk (or 2 c. half-and-half)
1 t. Creole seasoning

In a saucepan, melt butter over medium heat. Add onion, celery, and garlic, cook for 5 minutes, stirring occasionally. Stir in flour; cook for 2 minutes. Stir in chicken broth; cook for 10 minutes, stirring occasionally, until thickened. Add crab meat and shrimp. Stir in cream, milk, and Creole seasoning; cook for 10 minutes or until heated through, stirring occasionally. Serve immediately.

W. Thomas "Tom" Green, O.D. (a.k.a. Dr. Shel "Dom" Seen)
Cambridge Family Eye Care, Inc.

Main Dishes

De's Yummy Conviction Chicken

4 smallish organic chicken breasts
1 medium organic onion
6-8 stalks organic celery
Organic chicken broth
½ stick Hartzler butter
Sweet Hungarian paprika

Preheat oven to 350° F. Chop onion and celery medium/fine. Simmer in butter until just tender. Place chicken breasts in casserole lightly coated with organic cooking spray. Top chicken with onion/celery mixture. Add chicken broth to not-quite cover.

Sprinkle very liberal amount of paprika on top. Bake at 350° F, covered, for 45 minutes. Uncover and bake another 10-15 minutes until chicken is done.

Serve chicken breasts topped with vegetable mixture, salt, and pepper to taste, with mashed organic potatoes or yams.

De Felt
Cambridge Pet Advocate

Example sheds a genial light
Which men are apt to borrow,
So first improve yourself today
And then your friends tomorrow.

Coroner Jane's Juicy Spinach Meatballs

(An original recipe created in Jane Brickwall's kitchen by chief cook, Joan.)

1 lb. ground chuck
10 oz. pkg. frozen chopped spinach, thawed and drained
10-15 soda crackers
¼ c. Parmesan cheese, crushed, or crumbled
2 eggs, slightly beaten
Olive oil (several tablespoons)
1 small to med. onion, diced
1 clove garlic, smashed, peeled, and chopped
Soy sauce, low sodium
Garlic Expressions Vinaigrette® dressing *(or substitute any garlic Italian dressing/marinade)*
Salt and pepper to taste

Mix spinach, ground chuck, eggs, and Parmesan cheese together in a bowl. Add crackers, using 10 or more to a suitable consistency for meatballs. Salt and pepper to taste. Mix thoroughly with a spoon then use your hands until well mixed. Roll small meatballs about 1 inch in diameter and set aside.

In large sauce pan with tight fitting lid, pour several tablespoons olive oil, diced onion, and garlic. Cook on medium high heat, uncovered, until onions start to soften. Brown meatballs in pan, leaving enough space to turn. After meatballs are browned, cover pan, and reduce heat to medium low. After 15 minutes, add a splash or two of soy sauce; continue cooking on low heat, with lid on, for 30 minutes or until balls are cooked through.

Shortly before serving, add a splash of Garlic Expressions and cover again for another 5-10 minutes. Liquids should be completely absorbed by this time. Serve hot as a main course or use as hors d'oeuvres. Prep time: 10-15 minutes. Cook time: 45 minutes to 1 hour.

Janet M. Brockwell, M.D.
(a.k.a. Jane Brickwall)
Guernsey County Coroner

Contempt-of-Court Chicken Club Pizza

1 can (13.8 oz.) refrigerated pizza crust
¼ c. mayonnaise
½ c. ranch dressing, divided
1½ c. shredded cheddar cheese
1½ c. finely chopped cooked chicken
8 slices bacon, cooked and crumbled
1½ c. finely shredded lettuce
1 tomato, finely chopped

Heat oven to 400° F. Unroll pizza dough on baking sheet sprayed with cooking spray; press into 15x10-inch rectangle. Bake 10 minutes. Mix mayonnaise and ⅓ c. dressing; spread onto crust. Top with half the cheese, chicken, remaining cheese and bacon. Bake 5 minutes or until crust is deep golden brown and cheese is melted. Top with lettuce and tomatoes; drizzle with remaining dressing.

DENNIS DETTRA
SUPERINTENDENT, CAMBRIDGE CITY SCHOOLS

Homeless Hobo Habeus Corpus Stew

First, decide how many you want to feed. Then tear off a piece of foil (heavy duty) and place a raw hamburger patty in the center. Put onion, bell pepper, tomatoes, and potatoes on top. Salt and pepper to taste. Wrap foil up around meat and veggies and twist foil on top to close. You can put this in the oven and cook for about 30 minutes at about 400° F. You can also lay these on campfire coals or on a grill and cook that way. Under the viaduct, we use the campfire method.

BOBBY "KNUCKLES" DIFFENDORFER
KING OF THE ROAD

"LUNCH-LADY" CHILI BAKE

(Chef Edna Filbert's favorite recipe in "Murder by Muffin")

1 lb. ground beef
1 lg. onion, chopped
16 oz. can kidney beans, rinsed and drained
15¼ oz. can whole kernel corn, drained
15 oz. tomato sauce
14½ oz. can diced tomatoes, undrained
4 oz. can chopped green chilies
2 t. chili powder
1 t. salt
1 t. ground cumin
½ t. sugar
½ t. garlic powder

In a Dutch oven or soup kettle over medium heat, cook beef, onion, and green pepper until meat is no longer pink; drain. Add remaining ingredients; bring to a boil, stirring occasionally. Reduce heat; cover and simmer 10 minutes. Transfer chili to an ungreased 9x13-inch baking dish. Bake, uncovered, at 400° F. for 15-17 minutes. Serve with a corn muffin, green gelatin with fruit, and milk for a nostalgic meal. You'll think you're in school again!

BEVERLY JUSTICE
RAINY DAY WRITER

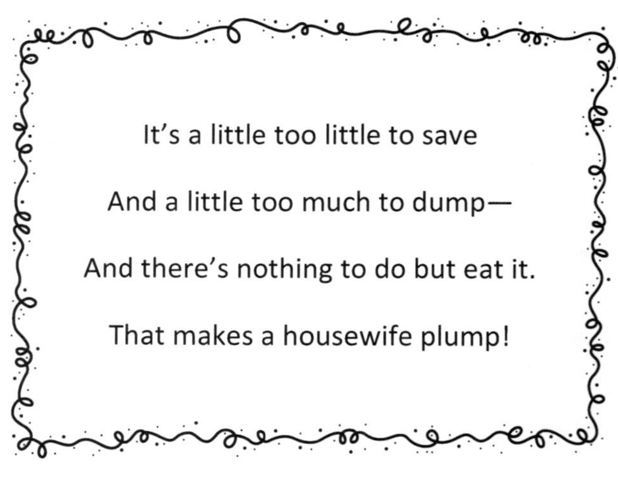

Crime of Passion Chicken Wings

2½ lbs. chicken wings, separated at joints (discard tips), lightly floured and lightly browned

To ¼ cup of soy sauce, add ½ cup water or chicken broth and 3 T. sherry or white wine.

To this mixture add:

½ t. poultry seasoning
1 t. dry mustard
½ t. ginger
2 T. brown sugar
2 or 3 green onions, cut in 1-inch pieces

Pour over browned chicken. Cover; heat to boiling; simmer 30 minutes. Uncover, simmer 15 minutes longer, basting frequently. Serve hot or cold. *(I usually double the recipe for a hungry gang). Note: May also be prepared using large chicken pieces for an entrée.*

Donna Lake Shafer
Rainy Day Writer

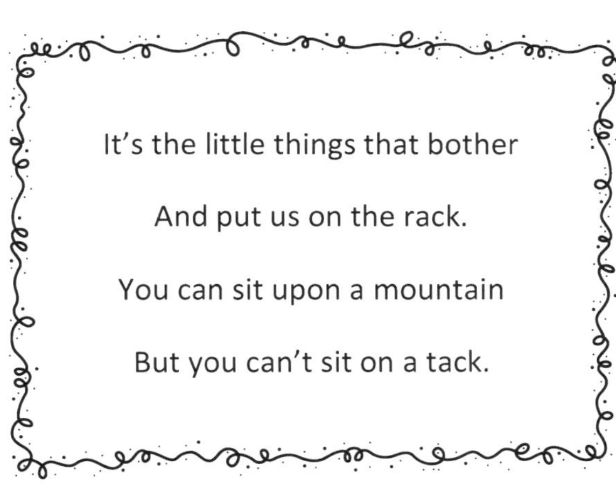

Awan's Pyramid Meatloaf

(Awan Massri's creative masterpiece in "An Egyptian Connection")

1½ lbs. ground beef *(camel meat may be substituted)*
1 egg
1 onion, chopped
1 c. milk *(cow or goat)*
1 c. dry bread crumbs *(or oats)*
Salt and pepper to taste
2 T. brown sugar
2 T. prepared mustard
⅓ c. ketchup

Preheat oven to 350° F. In a large bowl, combine beef, egg, onion, milk, and bread crumbs. Season with salt and pepper. Form into a pyramid shape and place in a lightly greased 9x13-inch baking dish. In a separate bowl, combine brown sugar, mustard, and ketchup. Mix well and pour over meatloaf. Bake at 350° F. for 1 hour.

Beverly Justice
Rainy Day Writer

Signature Steaks

4 ribeye steaks
Marinade:
1 c. Dijon mustard
½ c. honey
Salt to taste
Generous splash of Worcestershire sauce

Mix marinade ingredients in a bowl. Refrigerate, covered, 30 minutes. Preheat grill to medium-high. Coat steaks with chilled marinade. Grill on medium-high about 4 minutes each side for medium-rare. Serve whole or slice very thin.

Richard "Dick" Wayt *(a.k.a. Ricky Tate)*
Chief, Cambridge Police Department

Miles City Mayhem Pheasant

6 wild pheasant breasts

Stuffing:

1 finely chopped apple
2 diced scallions
2 c. cubed stuffing bread
1 egg
½ c.chicken stock
1 t. poultry seasoning

Orange Glaze:

½ c. white wine
1 c. orange juice
1 t. lemon juice
½ t. salt
½ t. lemon zest

Marinate breasts for 24 hours in light raspberry vinaigrette of your choice. Debone breasts and pound into thin medallions. Place ½ cup stuffing on each medallion. Roll up and place in oiled baking dish. Season to taste with salt and pepper. Drizzle with a little white wine and olive oil. Top each with 1-inch piece of smoked bacon held in place with a toothpick. Bake at 400° F. for 20-25 minutes. Bring glaze ingredients to a simmer and thicken with cornstarch mixed with cold orange juice. Drizzle glaze over baked breasts. Serve with fresh cooked spinach.

Dick Metheney
Rainy Day Writer

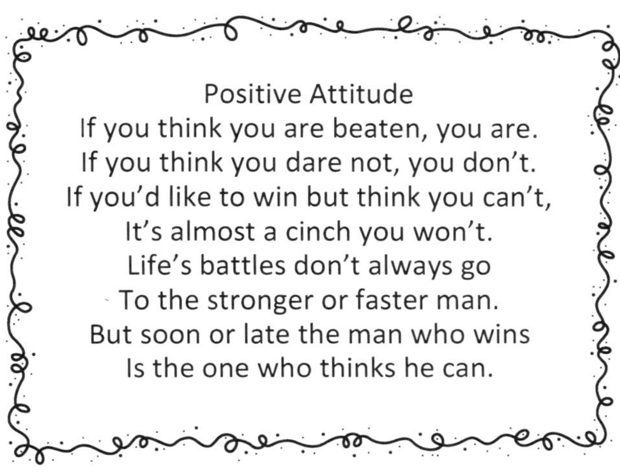

Positive Attitude
If you think you are beaten, you are.
If you think you dare not, you don't.
If you'd like to win but think you can't,
It's almost a cinch you won't.
Life's battles don't always go
To the stronger or faster man.
But soon or late the man who wins
Is the one who thinks he can.

DEADWOOD DICK'S JACKRABBIT SAUSAGE

(A specialty breakfast meat ala "The Clue Was Below the Tattoo")

3 lbs. ground jackrabbit
1 t. salt
½ t. white pepper
½ t. black pepper
½ t. thyme
½ t. freshly grated ginger
2 T. finely chopped fresh chives
2 T. finely chopped fresh parsley

Thoroughly mix all ingredients; form 3-oz. patties (approx. 5 patties per lb. or 3-inch diameter). Place in medium hot skillet with a little butter or olive oil. Sauté until thoroughly cooked (lightly browned). Serve with eggs, hash browns, and toast for a hearty breakfast.

DICK METHENEY
RAINY DAY WRITER

BEEF STROGANOFF ALA CRACKPOT

1½ lbs. beef for stew
2 T. butter
1½ c. beef bouillon
2 T. ketchup
1 small garlic clove, crushed
1 t. salt
8 oz. sliced mushrooms
1 medium onion, chopped
3 T. flour
1 c. sour cream
3-4 c. hot cooked noodles

Dredge beef in flour and salt. Melt butter in large skillet; add beef and onion. Cook over medium heat until browned. Place beef bouillon, ketchup, garlic, and mushrooms in crock pot and mix. Add cooked beef and onions. Cover and cook on low for 30-45 minutes. Do not let mixture boil. Serve over hot cooked noodles.

JERRY WOLFROM
RAINY DAY WRITER

Bratwurst Reuben Sandwiches

(Der Knödelmeister's specialty, from "Kraut Packs a Lot of Clout")

Sandwich Ingredients:

5 bratwurst links
1 pkg. hoagie/bratwurst rolls
1 pkg. sliced Swiss cheese (6-8 slices)
1 c. Thousand Island dressing

Sauerkraut Topping:

14.5 oz. sauerkraut, drained
¾ c. large red onion, sliced
½ c. sliced scallions, tops only
1-2 T. vegetable oil
½-¾ t. sugar, to taste
½-¾ t. garlic powder, to taste
2-3 dashes favorite hot sauce

Cut each bratwurst lengthwise, just two-thirds the way through. Gently flatten for quick and easy cooking. Cook bratwurst in skillet according to package directions. *Note: Cook time will be shortened.* Cook until no longer visibly pink. Place bratwurst to side, keeping it warm. Drain excess liquid from skillet. Add vegetable oil; return skillet to medium-high heat. Add sliced red onion and green pepper, sauté for 2-5 minutes until slightly tender. Add sauerkraut and gently heat together. Add seasonings and scallions; keep warm. Layer cooked bratwurst, sauerkraut mixture, Thousand Island dressing, and cheese on rolls. Serves 5.

Joy L. Wilbert Erskine
Rainy Day Writer

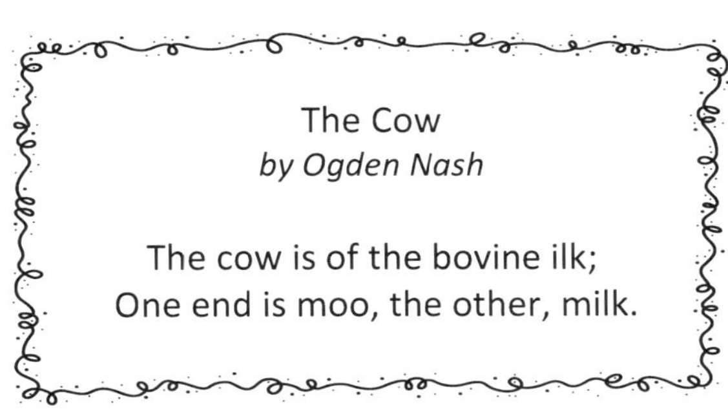

The Cow
by Ogden Nash

The cow is of the bovine ilk;
One end is moo, the other, milk.

The Prosecutor's Pastitsio

½ lb. elbow macaroni
½ can tomato paste
1 lb. ground beef
¾ c. water
1 large onion, chopped
3 eggs, beaten
¼ lb. butter
2 c. hot milk
1 t. cinnamon
½ c. grated cheese
Salt and pepper to taste

Cook macaroni in boiling salted water and drain. Sauté meat and onion in butter until lightly browned. Sprinkle with cinnamon, salt, and pepper. Add tomato paste mixed with water; simmer slowly until thick. Add hot milk to beaten eggs and combine with macaroni and meat. Pour ½ the mixture into a greased pan (approx. 7x11"). Sprinkle ½ the cheese on top, cover with the rest of the mixture and sprinkle with the remaining cheese. Bake in 325° F. oven for 30 minutes. Cut into squares and serve.

Kay Nicolozakes
Georgetown Vineyards

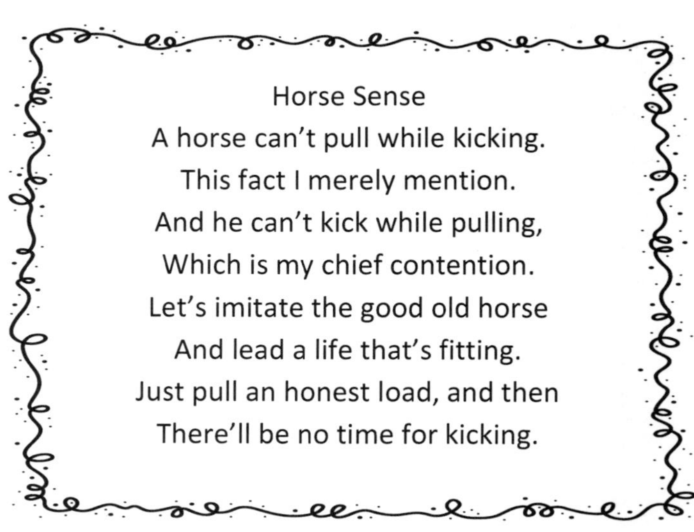

Horse Sense

A horse can't pull while kicking.
This fact I merely mention.
And he can't kick while pulling,
Which is my chief contention.
Let's imitate the good old horse
And lead a life that's fitting.
Just pull an honest load, and then
There'll be no time for kicking.

FOR A REALLY GOOD STEAK...

Check the parking lot at the Newcomerstown Elks Club on any Saturday night and you will find it jammed with cars from four adjoining counties. The reason? The club is open to the public on Wednesday and Saturday nights and the specialty is steak. Below are some tips from assistant chef Troy Lenzo for grilling a perfect steak.

Steaks should be grilled on an iron slab. The one at the Elks is nearly three inches thick, heated with five gas burners in different locations. On an ordinary backyard grill, the juice drips down on the flame, creating a smoky taste but also drying out an expensive cut of meat. Grilling steaks on a flat iron grill preserves the natural juices.

Pour a little oil on the grill then place room temperature steaks on it. Frozen, or even cold, steaks are a no-no. Also, the perfect taste comes from pre-aged meat, a process that takes from 10-21 days.

Immediately after the steak is on the grill, sprinkle Lowry's Steak Seasoning on both sides. Fry fast for a minute, then move the meat to a part of the grill with less heat. To get a perfect steak, use a thermometer to test for meat rareness. Never cut into a steak on the grill. Lenzo says steaks cooked medium are the most popular.

The Elks offers one-pound filet mignons, ½-pound filets, six-ounce filet petites, t-bones, New York strips, and rib eyes. One-pound filets and rib eyes are the most popular, according to Lenzo. Filets are purchased in two-foot "loaves," then custom cut for the perfect thickness, which is at least one and a half inches.

The steak kitchen at the Newcomerstown Elks was opened more than 40 years ago after the Heller Tool Company, a local plant, donated the heavy iron slab that became the grill.

JERRY WOLFROM
RAINY DAY WRITER

Cakes, Cookies, And Desserts

Gumshoe Gateau a L'Orange

1 box of Duncan Hines Golden Butter Cake Mix
½ c. salad oil
4 eggs
11 oz. can mandarin oranges with juice

Beat all together until oranges are no longer visible. Bake in 9x13-inch baking pan at 350° F. for 28-32 minutes. Let cool.

Topping:
9 oz. Cool Whip
1 small instant vanilla pudding
20 oz. can crushed pineapple with juice

Mix and spread on cake. Refrigerate.

Jo Sexton, President
Cambridge Area Chamber of Commerce

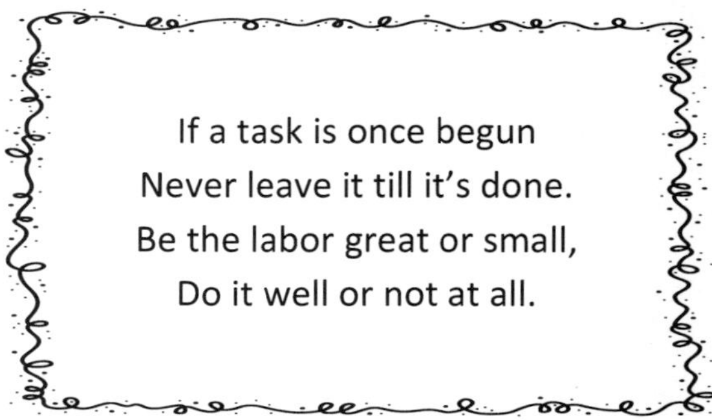

A.K.A. Amish Cookies

2 c. brown sugar
2 c. white sugar
1 c. butter
1 c. Crisco
4 eggs
2 t. vanilla
¼ c. milk

4½ c. flour
4 c. oats
2 t. baking powder
2 t. baking soda
1 t. salt
¼-½ c. chopped walnuts (opt.)

Mix together and chill. Roll into balls, dip in sugar, and flatten with fork. Bake at 400° F. for 8 minutes.

Ray Chorey
President and CEO
Southeastern Ohio Regional Medical Center

Nolo Contendre Nutty Dates

1 pkg. dates *(get them in the produce department)*
Cream cheese
Pecan halves

Snip off hard stem end of dates. Make thumbprint in dates and fill with cream cheese. Top with pecan half.

Donna Lake Shafer
Rainy Day Writer

Strawberry Subpoena Dessert

Angel food cake
2 pts. strawberries
1 sm. box vanilla instant pudding
1 c. milk
1 c. sour cream
Small container of Cool Whip
½ t. orange rind

Cut angel food cake in half; cut into bite size pieces. Combine pudding mix, milk, sour cream, Cool Whip, and orange rind in a bowl. In a glass bowl, layer ½ of cake pieces, ½ of sliced strawberries, and ½ of pudding mixture. Repeat layers with remaining angel food cake, strawberries and pudding mixture. I always add a few strawberries on top for decoration.

Tom Orr
(a.k.a. Strom Roarr)
Mayor of Cambridge

Roller Derby Pie

(A RollerGirlz fav from "Diva's Demise Is a Racy Surprise")

1 c. semisweet chocolate chips
1 c. English pecans or walnuts
2 eggs, beaten
1 c. sugar
1 stick butter, melted and cooled
½ c. + 2 T. flour
1 t. vanilla
Unbaked pie shell

Mix sugar and flour, add eggs; add butter. Add nuts, chocolate chips, and vanilla. Pour into unbaked pie shell. Bake at 350°F for 30 minutes. Test with toothpick. Pie should be chewy, but not runny.

Joy L. Wilbert Erskine
Rainy Day Writer

I Scream For Ice Cream

(An old family recipe that dates back some 100 years.)

6 eggs
½ gal. milk
1½ c. sugar
¼ c. dark Karo syrup

1 qt. half-and-half
OR 3 c. milk and 3 c. cream
1-3 t. vanilla

Beat well and pour into ice cream maker. Fill from ½ to 1 inch from top of can with milk. Crank 20 minutes.

Judge David A. Ellwood
Common Pleas Court

"Professor Plum Does It"

(Yogurt in Plum Wine)

½ c. frozen vanilla yogurt
2 T. (more or less to taste) plum wine *(I like Japanese Fuki brand best)*
Red raspberry sauce (purchased/made) (optional)
Chocolate sauce (purchased/made)

In a small dessert glass or dish, layer: yogurt, raspberry sauce over yogurt, and plum wine over raspberry sauce. Add a drizzle of chocolate sauce. Serve alone or with a sweet, like a cookie, brownie etc. Enjoy!

Dave Ogle
Scott-Ogle Realty Inc.

Life -Without-Parole Pumpkin Roll

1 c. sugar
¾ c. flour
1 t. salt
1 t. soda
1 t. cinnamon
⅔ c. pumpkin
3 eggs
½ c. chopped nuts

Mix first 5 ingredients. Add eggs and pumpkin. Mix well. Grease pan, then line with waxed paper on all sides. Sprinkle pan with nuts. Pour batter on top of nuts. Bake in a 15½x10-inch jelly roll pan for about 15 minutes.

Turn out on a linen towel, remove waxed paper, and sprinkle with powdered sugar. Then roll up into towel until completely cool. Unroll and fill. Place in foil and refrigerate.

Filling:
7 t. soft Land O' Lakes butter
1 t. vanilla
8 oz. pkg. cream cheese (room temperature)
1 c. powdered sugar

Mix until real creamy.

Jim Caldwell
Guernsey County Treasurer

Fruit-filled Meringue Cups

(A light dessert from Angus McHeilancoo in "Gallons of Macallan's)

3 egg whites
½ t. vanilla
¼ t. cream of tartar
¾ c. sugar
½ c. lemon pie filling
1 c. sliced strawberries
2 med. kiwifruit, peeled and sliced
½ c. fresh raspberries
⅓ c. mandarin oranges
⅓ c. cubed fresh pineapple

Place egg whites in a large (not plastic) mixing bowl; *let stand at room temperature for 30 minutes*. Beat egg whites, vanilla, and cream of tartar on medium speed until soft peaks form. *Gradually* beat in sugar on high, 1 tablespoon at a time, until stiff peaks form. Drop meringue into eight mounds on a parchment paper-lined baking sheet. Shape into 3-inch cups with the back of a spoon. Bake at 275° F. for 20-25 minutes or until set and dry. Turn off oven and *do not open door*; leave meringues in oven for 1 hour. Store in airtight container. Fill crisp, dry meringue cups with lemon pie filling just before serving. Top with fresh fruit. Yield: 2 dozen.

JOY L. WILBERT ERSKINE
RAINY DAY WRITER

I have a spelling chequer,
It came with my pea see.
It plane lee marks four my revue
Miss steaks I can knot sea.
I've run this poem threw it,
I'm sure your pleas to no.
Its let her perfect in it's weigh;
My chequeur tolled me sew.

THE CRITICS

"Wow! This book brings back some fond memories of the time when I was in my prime."—Jack the Ripper, White Chapel, London.

"I may file legal action against the Rainy Day Writers, who stole some of my shower curtain ideas. And they called me a 'Psycho?'"—Norman Bates, c/o Alfred Hitchcock, Bates Motel.

"What a great book. I wish I could have read it before I gave my father 40 whacks."—Lizzie Borden.

"There's a thin line between the plot in this book and 'Murder on the Orient Express.' With all due respect to Dame Agatha Christie, I like The Rainy Day Writers story best."—Hercule Poirot, Belgian detective.

"In this book, I don't know which is better, the murder mysteries or the recipes. Both are top quality and make the book worth far more than its $9.95 cover price."—Donald Trumpet, New York City.

"'The Southgate Parkway Murders' proves that when properly mixed, food and murder can be fun. We snacked all the way through it."—Dunkan Hines, Marie Calendar, Orval Reddensocker, and Mrs. Butterswort.

8746499R0

Made in the USA
Charleston, SC
11 July 2011